A STONE FOR AMER

D1320011

DISCARD

ALSO BY CONNIE CLAIRE SZARKE

DELICATE ARMOR
STONE WALL

A STONE FOR AMER

CONNIE CLAIRE SZARKE

HERON BAY PUBLISHING
Mound, MN
www.heronbaypublishing.com

Copyright © 2013 by Connie Claire Szarke

ISBN: 978-0-9885363-0-2

All rights reserved.

This book is a work of fiction. Names, characters, places, and incidents are the products of the author's imagination or are used fictitiously. Any resemblance to actual events or persons, living or dead, is entirely coincidental.

First Edition
Printed in the United States of America

Text is set in Perpetua
Book design and cover photo: Nancy Paddock

Published by Heron Bay Publishing, Mound, MN
www.heronbaypublishing.com

To Josh, Margot, and Leo; and to my father,
a grand raconteur who gave me the seeds for this story.

CONTENTS

"Whither is fled the visionary gleam?
Where is it now, the glory and the dream?"

—William Wordsworth

1

Know That He Mattered In This World

1986

IT FEELS GOOD to walk around this cemetery, stretch these old legs after such a long trip—more like a great journey at my age. Came all the way from Minneapolis. "Minnenapolis," as my brother calls it. Sure wish he could have come along with us—my daughter Cal and me. But Ray's in a nursing home in Sioux City, Iowa. Too bad he couldn't have been in on all this mess from the beginning. Ah, but that's water over the dam now. Or water under the bridge. Whichever way you want to look at it. Maybe some day I'll be able to tell my brother how it was for Uncle Amer. If he'll sit for it.

It's hot for September. I'm too warm in a suit and tie. For nearly an hour we've been wandering through this big old Swedish cemetery in search of a marker—one that I've tried to visualize for some time. I can tell you right now, I'm not giving up. If I could look at my uncle lying in that dirt basement, I sure as hell can shuffle around these headstones until I find him. I told Cal we're not leaving until I do.

I was sixteen when Dad and I went out West to claim Amer's body. Be eighty-five next birthday.

Well, you might say, that was a long time ago. True. But I'm still bitter about the way he died. For some things in life, time has no business figuring in. The way I see it, there aren't any limits. A fellow can hurt just as much over an age-old wound as he would from yesterday's sorrow.

Cal and I drove here to Rockford, Illinois, in part to visit relatives, though more of them are planted in this cemetery than live in town. Mainly, I'm here after all these years to see that my Uncle Amer's grave has been done up right. As it should be. As promised.

Why did it take me so long to return to Rockford? Cal and I talked about that during the long drive. Talked about all the usual reasons people put off taking trips, making pilgrimages. The years peel by when a fella's out there earning a living, raising a family, taking care of a home. That's how it was for Emily and me. Our daughters. My work at the courthouse. Looking after Mother. Travel was a luxury during the war years. After that, the decades slipped by like northern pike through rips in a landing net.

It felt a little strange to see Hannah and Nellie when we pulled up to their house. Haven't seen these cousins since Mother's funeral back home in Masterton. That sad and embarrassing day when my brother Ray and his wife ransacked Mother's house. Didn't bother to join the rest of us after the service. I ought to be over it by now, but that's one thing still sticks in my craw.

With little in common, my cousins and I had lost touch. Besides, I didn't care to discuss the rift between my brother and me. Still don't. As for their dads (my other uncles), they must have set some kind of stone for Amer—maybe even a Lindstrom marker to include Grandma and Auntie. Now, if we can just find them....

On the way here, Cal reminded me of my sudden decision to make this trip. Reminded me of what I'd said that afternoon while we were at the Leech Lake powwow up in northern Minnesota.

"Something resonated with you that day," she said, driving my '85 Cadillac as if it were a racecar. "I could tell."

"Maybe so," I admitted, leaning over to glance at the speedometer. "Slack up, Callie. You're going too fast."

"I'm only doing sixty-five," she said, easing off the gas pedal.

"Well, we didn't just hop into a car and go places in those

days," I said, skipping back to my reasons for not making this trip sooner. "Not like now. Folks ramming around all over the place, ignoring the speed limits. Not like in my day. We conserved on gas and tires."

"Maybe we should have walked to Rockford, huh, Dad? Like Ocheyedan. Remember Ocheyedan?"

"Unforgettable," I said, relaxing against my seatback, feeling loose as a sack of fresh oats. "Your mother and Liz thought we looked like a couple of vagabonds marching down Main Street."

"Yeah, and when it came time to hug us, they acted as though they needed a pair of clothespins."

"Hah! Good for what ailed them."

When Cal was twelve or thirteen, we strapped on backpacks and hiked from Masterton to Ocheyedan, Iowa. It took us three days to reach our destination, meandering along gravel roads, across bean and cornfields, around lakes, sleeping under the stars. A wonderful time. When we finally paraded into that little town, Emily and Liz were there, waiting to pick us up.

"That was a hell of a lot of fun, wasn't it, kiddo?"

"Damn right, Dad."

"Yep, that was some hike." I reclined my car seat and settled in for a little snooze. "Keep her below sixty, Cal. We'll get there in plenty of time."

"I'll think about it," she said, flashing a sly grin.

Truth be told—one that I'll never admit to my family, although they're likely on to it—the main reason I decided to come back to Rockford is that, as the saying goes, I'm feeling my mortality. Emily and I won't be returning to California this winter. And I've made a mental list of things I need to do before my time is up. This trip made the top of the list.

Throughout the years, I've never really thought about Uncle Amer lying in the ground, though I was here when they lowered him. As long as I could tell his story, he lingered above good old terra firma like a spirit, in all his likeness, still laboring in the fields, tending the livestock, singing and playing his violin. Even Cal used to talk about him as if he were still alive. She was a youngster when she discovered a trunk full of Amer's things in the storeroom of our cottage on Lake Shetek. For the longest time, she only read his early letters. Put off opening that final correspondence. The witness testimonies. The coroner's report.

I let my thoughts drift back once again to that afternoon at the Leech Lake powwow near Federal Dam. What was it about the steady beat of that drum? From the moment we entered the gate, I felt it inside my chest. That deep, constant rhythm of the drum. Those powerful dancers with the painted faces. The elders who wore their hair in long, gray braids and sang those same notes, their voices starting high on the scale, descending to a lower pitch, then hovering, hovering until the birds of your mind took flight and the Indians paused for another breath in order to begin again. And always, the beating of the drum.

What was it about that afternoon? All I know is that was the day when something told me it was time to put things to right. Wrap up any business left undone. Mend fences with my brother. Make sure Uncle Amer was laid to rest in proper fashion, with a stone to mark his place.

And that's what this trip is all about.

I wanted Emily and Liz to come along but they declined. Some big shindig in Masterton with the ladies from Emily's 500 Club. All still kicking, except for Hulda Swenson. I don't know what got the better of her. My guess is that it had something to do with the long ago death of her little daughter, when Doc Nelson screwed up big time after a routine tonsillectomy. I have a hunch the pain and bitterness of losing that beautiful child took its final toll. And, as Callie used to say, "Hulda Swenson couldn't ever get another baby."

Anyhow, Liz and her hubby, Brian, are driving over from Wisconsin to take Emily back to our hometown. I'd like to see my old friends and neighbors again, especially Carl Ryan and Ted Claussen. Used to hunt ducks with them. I might have gone along, but Callie and I had already planned this trip to Rockford.

Besides, I'm not so keen on going back to Masterton

just yet, since the powers-that-be destroyed our stately courthouse. Replaced it with some wimpy building at the head of Main Street. Just imagine! Maywood County courthouse, built in 1891, placed on the National Register of Historic Buildings in 1977. And four years later, that gang found some excuse to tear it down. (The almighty dollar most likely crowned the black heart of that deal.) At least they couldn't rip out my memory of the place: the clock tower dome, the yellow brick and limestone arched portico, the sounds of farm boots crossing the heavy chain- and leather-linked tread inside the entry. The smells of ledgers and ink, and cigarette smoke drifting up from the basement. Those stone steps worn concave. My office on the left with its lofty, crenellated ceiling. And leading upstairs to the courtroom curved the long, ornate banister made shiny from a century of hands—smooth as the skin on a young bullhead. For twenty-three years I kept the books inside that building—golden warm on the coldest of winter mornings.

Oh, I'll go back to Masterton one day, but not until I'm good and ready.

As for our grandkids, Josie and Brent, why we hardly see them now that they're all grown up and leading busy lives. Typical of young people these days. They're good kids, just not always interested in us old folks. Although, I'm pleased to say that Josie has recently paid some attention to our family history, especially Amer's. Some day, we'll bring her to Rockford, show her the house on State Street, where I was born. And McNeil Road, named after Mother's Uncle Abe. I'll bet she'd like to see that big building that went up in a barn-raising when I was in fourth grade and we visited Rockford. And the old schoolhouse. But it's not a school any more. Someone turned it into a house. Times change.

This time, it's just the two of us, Callie and me. Besides, as Emily made sure to mention before sending us on our way, "It's fitting for you and Callie to make this trip by yourselves."

In a way she's right. Cal has always taken a sharp interest in what happened to Uncle Amer. Grew up hearing me tell his story since she was old enough to understand most of it. The other day she asked me to set the whole thing down on paper. I'd like to oblige. In fact, I tried several times to scribble a few memories. But I'm a better talker than writer. Always have been.

Lately, though, when I get to the end, there seems to be something missing. I told the family I need to see Amer's grave. Witness some tangible evidence. Make sure that all who pass by can read his name and know that he mattered in this world.

Here is how Cal and I picture his tombstone:

Amer Lindstrom

Born 1880 • Died 1919

2

A Place Called God's Country

MY COUSINS HANNAH AND NELLIE, here in the cemetery with us, live in Rockford town. Besides my brother and me, they're the only relatives left out of that whole batch of Lindstroms. We already paid our respects in the newer section where their parents are buried under elaborate black headstones with the shapes of plows and furrows etched on them. But here, most of the fog-colored tombstones require better eyesight than I have, though who'd want to admit that. It's not easy making out names and dates carved in soft, gray-white stone grown over with dark moss and yellow lichens.

During the better part of a hundred years, rain, sleet, hail, snow, wind, and a hot sun have worn the lettering to shallow troughs. Shadowy hints of who lies buried beneath and how old they were when felled by disease or old age or murder or heaven knows what else fate had in store for them. No amount of squinting through my bifocals at these chalky blocks of stone reveals the answers. Turns out most of the lettering is in Swedish.

"My, oh my!" Hannah's sharp voice startles me. "It's like trying to decipher hieroglyphs, don't you know."

"Yah, yah," Nellie answers.

Oh, these women. How they lag behind, inching past each marker and rough gray slab as if they had all the time in the world. Can't they remember where Amer is? They should be able to lead us directly to him. After all, they come here often enough. Oh, well, they're elderly, so what can I say? Hell, I might as well just stand here for a while and look around.

The entry is impressive—a tall, ornate wrought-iron gate with the name Rockford Swedish Cemetery welded at the top. Backwards now, from my vantage point. A car path circles the perimeter with two intersecting roads, like an oddly-shaped pie cut into quarters.

The trees are huge in this old section. Majestic. Of course, it's no surprise that they're much taller than they were seventy years ago. But how those maple and cottonwood branches sprawl across the firmament. And how the spruce and arborvitae stand like giant sentinels, waving their long arms, towering over the graves. I may be hard of hearing, but I can still make out the shushing sound of the wind tracking through these boughs. And I can smell autumn in the air.

Cal takes my arm and rests her head against my shoulder while we pause before a cluster of infants' graves. Without saying, we remember Billy—Emily's and my baby boy who died in his crib several years before Cal was born. I wish he could have known Liz and Callie, his big and little sisters. And I wish to high heaven we could have known him. I often wonder what little Billy would have been like and the sort of man he would have become. What turn would our lives have taken had he lived?

"William," Hannah announces, "I feel faint in this heat. I go sit down, yah, yah."

Callie snickers (not in a mean way) and whispers her own version of "Yah, yah," as we watch Hannah totter across the dirt road that circles the cemetery and wilt onto a bench in the shade of the largest cottonwood tree in this old section. My God, you'd think she was Greta Garbo the way she presses the back of her hand against her forehead. And her accent is so thick you could ladle it up with a slotted spoon and not lose a bit of it.

Nellie is easier to understand and not so delicate. Not very bright, either, if you ask me. A lot like her father—

fixed in opinions, short on imagination. She reminds me of a big old robin, cocking her head as she moves from stone to stone, poking at the crab grass with her cane.

"Where the hell is he, Nellie?" I loosen my tie—and not just because of the heat. "He was supposed to go in next to Grandma and Auntie."

Nellie grumbles something about "cuss words," stoops over a patch of ground, peers through her bifocals at a pair of small metal plaques, and shouts as if we're all a mile away, "Here they are! Yoo-hoo! Over here, everyone! I found them!"

Hannah gets up too quickly from her bench and staggers toward us, crossing the narrow road like a woman come unhinged.

I quickly join Nellie and lean over for a closer look at two tiny plaques barely peeking up at us through thick grass. "Unacceptable," I mutter, trying to edge the growth away with the toe of my dress shoe. "See here, Cal? Grandma and Auntie aren't even properly marked. These are the same old temporaries that were dropped in right after they died. I remember seeing these as a kid."

Callie's jaw drops. "Is this it?" she asks. "Is this all there is? Not even a last name?"

I kick once more at the earth around two bronze squares where grass cuticles have taken over. Damned stuff, all matted and thick. I can barely make out the tiny lettering:

| MOTHER ERNESTINA 1899 | DAUGHTER EDNA 1900 |

To the left of these, there is only sod. No other marker. Just sod. Like a two-person search party, Callie and I shuffle through the grass, hoping to find something more.

"Oh, Dad," says Cal, focusing on the ground. "I don't see anything."

"What the...? There's nothing here for Amer!"

"Sakes alive, William," growls Hannah. "You'll wake the dead."

"I don't care. We had an agreement. If Dad and I brought him back, your folks would set a proper tombstone. What the hell happened?"

"Really, Will. You needn't cuss."

"I can't believe this. No stone for Uncle Amer?"

"Oh, it's all such a puzzle," says Nellie, pursing her thin lips as if sucking on a sourball. That one has always looked as though she's just been spooned a healthy dose of castor oil.

"You shouldn't blame us," she whines. "We were only young girls when this happened. And don't forget, times were hard back then. You know that, Will. And how's a come you never bothered to return in all these years? Until now?"

"Yah, yah," pipes Hannah, blotting her temples with a starched white hanky edged in pink lace. "I'm afraid we haven't given much thought to this part of the cemetery since our own folks passed. It's all we can do to set out flowers for them once a year."

Is she that frail, for heaven's sake? I focus on Hannah's features to determine if what she says is true and if, in some small way, she's allowing me my own reasons for not having come back to Rockford, until today. I stare at her clear blue eyes and innocent half smile that reveal nothing out of the ordinary. And those dabs of rouge and powder, like white and pink dust, caked over soft wrinkles in the heat of the day. That large, shiny nose and stout frame. Yah, yah, she's always had a poker face, that one. And I can't resist saying:

"Well, after all, your folks were supposed to see to it that Amer got a suitable burial. That was the deal." I yank off my necktie and mop my brow with the fresh handkerchief Emily tucked into my breast pocket earlier this morning.

"Hell, their folks were too damned Scotch to buy the stones," I whisper to Cal—a little too loudly, I guess, because she puts a finger to her lips.

"Hush, Dad, they'll hear you."

"Well, some Swedes hold their purse strings pretty damned tight to the vest," I mutter, shrugging off my suit jacket. "Shoot! They can't hear me. I don't think there's much juice left in their batteries."

Once again, I poke around on the grass with the toe of my shoe. "How could they just leave it this way? I guess

Amer might as well have been lowered into a pauper's grave, the way the sheriff said, when no one claims the body."

Looking a little tired around the eyes, Cal shakes her head. "Oh, Dad," she says. "I'm so sorry. I'm as disappointed as you are."

"It's been seventy years," I say loudly enough for all to hear, "and I'd like some answers. Uncle Frank and Uncle Ed were supposed to plan the funeral service. If we paid the undertaker back in Montana, plus our travel expenses bringing Amer home, they'd take care of the rest. A respectable casket, a decent plot. Hell, wouldn't you think that would have included a tombstone? Even a simple one, for Christ's sake—those chea…"

"This is the spot. I'm sure of it," says Hannah, who has wandered back to where Callie and I are standing. "This is where Grandma and Auntie are. As I recall, Amer got put in alongside them, here on the left." She points an arthritic finger at a piece of ground next to the curb.

Cal and I scour the plot one more time, on the chance that we've missed some small marker hidden in the crabgrass.

Nellie takes a little pair of shears from her purse, bends over, and tries to clip the coarse, thick grass away from our grandmother's plaque, emitting little grunting sounds with each gouge.

"Oh, for heaven's sake, Nell," says Hannah in a voice tinged with sarcasm. "Those scissors are so dull you could ride to town on them."

Cal laughs into her fist. And I can't help but chuckle.

With great effort, Nellie stands. Clutching her tiny weapon and waving it high in the air, she tips backwards for a moment, until she can find her equilibrium. Hard to believe these are the same cousins who used to scramble up haymow ladders, swim in oat bins, and gallop their ponies across the fields like Annie Oakley. I, myself, may have slowed down a bit, but not that much.

"So, this is all he got—this little patch of ground," I blurt out. "Not even a temporary, a bronze plaque like Grandma's and Auntie Edna's. I don't like this one bit. To think that a man who worked acres and acres of land all his life should end up in a plot that seems barely large enough for a child's coffin. And no marker! After what my dad and I went through to bring him home, for Christ's sake."

I feel light in the head. My heart skips a beat.

"Dad's right," Cal says in a stern voice, moving in close, ready to bolster me if need be. "He and Grandad did their part. There should be something here for Amer."

Taking shallow breaths, I make an effort to hide my sadness as I look from Cal to Nell and Hannah, remembering when Amer first came to live with us on our farm near Hadley, in Southwestern Minnesota—a place we called God's Country.

3

Dressed Like a Hussy

GOD'S COUNTRY—THE YEAR, nineteen-aught-six, when Uncle Amer came to live with us. My brother and I were little shavers. I was born in aught-three and Ray in aught-two.

Amer had a higher pitched voice than our dad and the occasional mannerisms of Stan Laurel, including the vacant twinkle in his eyes, which made it all the funnier when he told his jokes. From the time we could understand language, he'd have us gather 'round, teach us songs from the operas, read us grown-up books. And tease us. At some level we knew he was kidding, yet we believed everything he said. Even the times he'd ruffle our hair and tell us that Ray, as a newborn, was found in a slough near Bear Lake Woods, hanging around a flock of mallards, until he could figure out which one he wanted to fly in on. I'd ask,

"If my brother came out of a slough on the back of a quacker, where'd I come from, Uncle Amer?" And he'd say,

"You, Willie-boy? Why, you swam all the way through Lake Summit on the tail of a Great Northern Pike."

When I told Uncle Ed (Nellie's father) that my brother and I had come into this world on a duck and a fish, he stared at us, slack-jawed, as if we really had.

Mother and Dad and Uncle Amer made life exciting for Ray and me. For sure, there was hard work to be done on the farm, starting at a young age—six, seven. We had to feed the dogs, gather corncobs for Mother's cook stove, collect eggs from the coop and from the secret places around the farmyard, wherever the chickens decided to lay: inside the machine shed, beneath a tractor, next to a tree in the oak grove. That was like going on a treasure hunt. We went with Dad to check the traps he'd set around Bear Lake Woods, and brought back muskrats, beavers, and an occasional mink. Dad skinned them out, then stretched and nailed their hides to the gray wooden siding of another old shed that doubled as a garage.

Away from the farmyard, next to an open field, Dad and Uncle Amer fixed up a place for trap shooting. Hunters came from all over Maywood County to practice their leads on clay birds. Hunting dogs, especially Labradors and Chesapeakes, our own included, sat nearby, wide-eyed, muscles aquiver, ready for a command. It didn't take them long to realize it would be a day of rest and play while their sharp-eyed shooters competed for trophies and pooled prize money.

"Pull!" called the men in varying pitches. Then came the shotgun blast and clay pigeon fragments raining down from a summer-blue sky with white clouds high above. Sometimes, a black and yellow disc flew far across the field, untouched. A miss like that didn't happen very often.

You could close your eyes and know which man was going to shoot by the sound of his "Pull!" Uncle Amer had a distinctive call, bordering on the musical. "Pull!" he'd sing out in his tenor voice.

Occasionally, in early evening, my mother joined us, wearing a pair of Dad's baggy pants and a work shirt, her long, wavy black hair pulled back and secured with combs. Mother was a pretty good shot. It sounded funny, though, to hear her soprano voice call, "Pull!"

In the fall, the men and their dogs came back to hunt pheasants in our cornfields and to fill out on their limits of ducks and geese from nearby sloughs: mallards, teal, redheads, canvasbacks, Canadian honkers.

As soon as my brother and I were able to raise a shotgun in a single smooth motion, we stood before our posts and called out in as deep a voice as we could muster, "Pull!" We also took turns at the trap, springing clay pigeons for shooters who rarely missed.

Ray and I competed against each other, kept a running tally from one shoot to the next. Usually, he'd go off someplace to sulk. But with Dad and Uncle Amer, there was no competition; they were equals. Between them, they filled the tack room shelves in our barn with every kind of prize you could win for trap shooting in those days—the early 1900s: framed certificates with curlicue handwriting in black ink faded brown, hand-stitched blue ribbons, carved balsa wood trophies, bronze medals strung on leather thongs.

When Uncle Amer sauntered across the farmyard with his shotgun or stood off to one side of the shooting range, waiting his turn, he always seemed a little vulnerable to me. But as soon as he stood at his post, snapped that twelve-gauge to sight, and leaned into position, he was as stanch and unwavering as the rest of the men.

Now, as I turn away from this little patch of graveyard grass, recalling how Amer had once lived and labored on great stretches of land at home and in Montana, I can't help but shout:

"Listen here! Of all the family, why is it that Amer's the only one who went forgotten?"

Hannah and Nellie shrug and continue gazing at the two existing plaques and at the ground next to them.

"Hell, they can't even look at me, Callie. The sins of their fathers—that's what this is all about. A carry-over. Same damned attitude drifted down into the next generation."

"Dad, I feel as badly as you do. I thought for sure we'd find a stone for him—a really nice marker. Maybe we should arrange for one ourselves. What do you think?"

"Thirty-nine years old. Gave it everything he had. If only we'd known sooner.... He was such a friendly sort. Shouldn't have had an enemy in the world."

"Well, your folks were awfully protective of him, Will," says Hannah, finally looking in my direction. "He had to try going it alone some time."

"Yes," Nellie sighs, "but he was always a little...I don't know...peculiar. That's what my mother used to say. So peculiar. They never really cared for the way..."

"What are you talking about?" I feel a surge in blood pressure. "They never cared for what? What's that supposed to mean?" A little woozy, I take hold of Cal's arm.

"I only meant..."

"For Christ's sake, Nell, he never hurt a living thing! He worked damn hard, hired out to the neighbors when they needed an extra hand. We were lucky to have his help on the farm. Everyone in Leeds Township liked Amer, rooted for him when he played baseball with the Hadley Buttermakers. One of the best pitchers they ever had."

"Well, that may be, but..."

"And he was good to us kids. If we dared complain about those long hot days in the fields, we never got a scolding. Oh, we got plenty of that from our folks, but never from Uncle Amer. He always made us laugh. Had a knack for turning hard work into a game, especially during corn picking time. You remember those days, harvesting corn by hand."

"Who could forget?" Hanna snorts. "Suffering under a hot sun. Tough leather wrist huskers lopping off one ear at a time. It was no picnic."

"I remember that story," says Cal in a bright voice. "Uncle Amer painted a bull's-eye on the wagon's bang board so you could keep score. Like playing darts with ears of corn."

Another thread of memory drifts by me. "Yup. And Old Bessie and Fanny pulled the wagon through the cornrows all by themselves. No driver, no commands—they knew how to set a pace that kept up with ours."

Talking about those years, and casting aside Nellie's comment about Amer, brings back the sounds and smells of our farm. The rustle of brittle cornstalks brushing up against the wagon, a skittering pheasant—wings whistling as he takes to the air, the clunk of dried ears striking the bang board. A pale blue sky with mounded clouds on the distant horizon. Field dust coating the sweaty horses whose shaggy hooves flip forward and back, crunching tough roots as the team plods along under a scorching sun.

"Mixed breeds, they were," I tell the ladies. "Bessie and Fanny, part Shire and part Percheron. A fine pair."

"We had draft horses like that," says Hannah in a sing-song voice, as if trying for a one-up. "Duke and Sadie. Bessie was one of our milk cows, but we always called her in with, 'Here, Boss, Come, Boss.'"

"Everyone had a 'Bossie' in those days," I mutter.

Nellie's eyes narrow as she points her cane at me. "Amer might have made things fun for you and Ray, but don't forget how he acted during that Halloween party we went to one year."

"What do you mean?"

"He had a tendency to take things a little too far, according to Mother and Daddy—showing up at the sale barn dressed like a hussy."

"Of course. All decked out in a mask and wig. So what?"

"A long, blond wig. And balloons tucked under some dress he borrowed from your mother. It was grotesque. That's what Mother said. Why, he was practically...I don't know...he looked like a..."

"It was a masquerade, Nell. Everybody wore a costume. A few of the women dressed like men. Why don't you make something out of that?"

"To think he got by with using the women's restroom! Then laughed about it afterward. And the way he walked? My land!"

Nellie stands cockeyed, one hand on her hip like Mae West about to suggest, "Why don't you come up and see me sometime?"

"Nell, your lingo hasn't changed one whit since you were a girl. You sound like an over-the-fence gossip. So what if he played his part? So what?"

"Our folks thought it was disgusting, didn't they, Hannah? Why, I remember Mother and Daddy saying..."

"Hell, you remember things you have no business remembering! He was just having fun, making people laugh."

I don't care for this shift in conversation. Feeling a little woozy again. And Cal looks confused. She hasn't heard these details. I've never brought them up. Wouldn't have known quite how to do that anyhow, and so....

"What are you talking about?" she asks.

"Nothing. Not a damned thing. Amer was just as I've told you, Cal, a fun-loving, hard-working man who shouldn't have had an enemy in the world. And now this." I point at the ground. "Inexcusable!"

Hannah raises a hand like a teacher quieting her class. "I think we should rest for a spell, yah, yah." She shepherds us across the narrow road, toward a pair of sturdy benches.

It takes my cousins forever to sit—such a big production of snapping open their purses, fishing out large handkerchiefs for the occasion and placing them just right on the curved slats of a recently-varnished bench. They ease themselves down and fuss with their skirts, arranging the folds until they look like drooping peach and lime green poppies—if there are such things. Nellie sits as straight as a headstone, hands clutching her purse as if she were riding a city bus in a rough neighborhood. Hannah pats the space between, inviting Callie to join them. Good sport that she is, Cal backs up to the bench and laughingly wedges herself between the two elderly women. Hannah chuckles and wraps an arm around Cal's shoulders. Nellie manages one of her castor oil smiles.

To these old eyes, my daughter still looks like a girl. Resembles me, I think: shiny hair, almost black (like mine used to be), olive skin, eyes the color of a northern lake. You'd never know we're Scandinavian. What is her age now? Forty-two, I believe. Yes, forty-two last June. Doesn't seem possible.

At times, she still acts like a kid. My fishing buddy. Of course, we haven't been out on a lake since we got caught in that awful rainstorm up north. With all the doctoring I've had to do, my tackle box hasn't seen the light of day in some time. The old Johnson 10-horse hangs from a crosspiece in one corner of the garage and my Crestliner sits on its trailer, covered with a tarp against the snow and cold, which will come as surely as the geese and ducks return in spring. Sad, though, to see a boat dry-docked, even in winter. She sure did her best by us, getting us around the big waters during that storm on Leech Lake when I wasn't sure we'd make it back to shore alive.

On our way to Rockford, Cal and I reminisced about our adventure on Leech. How she bailed water like the very devil, second-guessing my change in direction, wondering if I knew what I was doing at the throttle. We can laugh about it now—that wall of water charging at us from across the bay, a mean sky behind it, those sudden whitecaps and monstrous rollers breaking over the stern of our small fishing boat. I'm glad Cal didn't let that experience deter her from going out on the water again. But then, I knew she wouldn't.

She seems to enjoy being the pampered girl today, acquiring a greater sense of the half of her that's Swedish. Got a good dose of the Old Country upon our arrival in Rockford. Hannah and Nellie welcomed us with bosomy hugs and a wonderful lunch of homemade meatballs, limpa bread, and rice pudding with lingonberry sauce. Hard to beat a meal like that. Cal's eyes sparkled as the four of us sat down together amid old treasured plates and silver service. And my cousins' lilting accents. I felt like a boy again, minding my manners at the same lace-covered cherry wood table set with the same fragile china. And that herd of red, blue, and yellow Dala horses standing stiff-legged in the center. Some things never change from one generation to the next. Some good, some not so good.

Now, sitting on the bench beneath the cottonwood tree, Hannah smiles and playfully butts shoulders with Cal.

"Yah, yah. I'm so glad you came along with your papa,"

she says. "We like getting to know you."

Yes, Hannah is a lot like her father, Frank—able to find humor in her days, managing to give out a little warmth.

And then there's Nellie—old sobersides, rigid as a fence post, her mouth like a Vise-Grip. Must run in that side of the family. Uncle Ed, her father, seldom cracked a smile. And neither did her mother.

"What will you choose when the time comes?" Nellie asks of no one in particular. "Burial or cremation?"

Callie frowns slightly at a subject she shouldn't as yet have to consider.

"A hell of a thing to bring up, Nell." I scowl at my cousin. "I don't know. Haven't thought about it." (Actually, I have. But I don't care to discuss it.)

"Hannah?" continues Nellie, as if conducting a seminar. "How about you?"

"Oh, cremation, yah, yah." Hannah's head bobs like a pigeon.

"But it's so final," Nellie says with a shiver.

Raising an eyebrow, Hannah tisk-tisks and says, "Well, old girl, do you think everyone's going to rise again? Stand around and clap their hands?"

Nellie purses her thin lips and twiddles her thumbs. "My, oh my. Guess we won't know till we get there."

I snort at their lingo and lean over to contemplate the lavender and yellow wildflowers threading themselves through the wrought iron base of my bench. As much as I've appreciated my cousins' hospitality since our arrival, I've never been able to abide a babbling old biddy.

After casting off my irritation, I look up to see what the wind is doing. Cal, trying to suppress a complicit smile, glances overhead, alert to the strong breeze pushing through big pines. The wind stirs up the cottonwood leaves, making them tremble like a thousand fluttering hands—an audience applauding a stellar performance. I prefer to imagine that the applause is for Uncle Amer and the fact that nothing could have prevented him from boarding that west-bound train to Montana.

Lingering here in this cemetery brings to mind, not only Uncle Amer, but other family members long dead. Family members whose behavior and untimely deaths greatly affected their five sons, including my father and Uncle Amer.

"What do you know about August?" I ask my cousins. "The old Swede who was our grandfather?" All my life, I've wondered why he lit out, abandoning his family—a family of six, including our dads, Uncle Amer, Uncle Reno, and daughter Edna.

"I never heard much talk," says Hannah, "except that one day he just up and left."

"Daddy refused to discuss it," says Nellie, "so we gave up asking. Awful, just awful for a man to leave his family like that, and having so many sons who needed him."

Of course, all that happened around 1898, years before my cousins and my brother and I were born. But Grandfather August was the talk of our family all the while I was growing up. Grandma thought he'd gone back to Sweden, until one of the boys spotted him two counties over—with another "wife" and a second herd of children.

Learning about her husband's secret life was more than Grandma Ernestine could endure. She never smiled again and died within a year. That left young Edna in charge of her five brothers. Till she got the influenza and died shortly after her seventeenth birthday. Those bronze markers across the way belong to them: Ernestine and Edna.

After that, the boys parted company. As my dad and Uncle Amer used to say, "We all drifted away like sagebrush before the wind."

Frank and Ed wandered around the Dakotas for a few years before settling in Illinois. Uncle Reno, as rumor had it, set himself up as a ladies' man in San Francisco, shot craps, and frequented opium dens in Chinatown. And then there was Amer, who farmed with my dad before striking out on his own. All different kinds of sagebrush.

"What really happened to Uncle Amer?" asks Hannah. "We were never as close to him as you and your brother were. Over the years, we only heard bits and pieces."

"My folks," chimes Nellie, "blamed it on that part of the

country—too wild, they said. Mother said he never should have gone to Montana. 'A place like that?' she said. 'Why, it wasn't safe. He should have stayed at home where everybody knew him.'"

"Well, he's home now, Nellie," says Hannah, pulling a face as she motions toward his supposèd grave across the road.

"Sempty years," I murmur, pronouncing the number the way my mother used to say it. "Tucked under that corner piece of sod. And not one mark to let the world know who he was."

"Tell us, Will," says Nellie. "We'd like to hear more about him, wouldn't we, Hannah?

"Yah, yah. But wouldn't it be more comfortable if we went back to the house?" Hannah shifts her ample behind on the bench in an exaggerated way. "I could put on the coffee and then…"

"Nope, we're gonna stay right where we are." I nod at the gravesites across the way and reach into my suit coat pockets for a bundle of yellowed envelopes—letters from Amer—and for my pipe and tobacco. "Right where we are," I repeat, tamping a bowlful. "It's the least we can do for him. No, siree, I won't be telling Amer's story over lace doilies and teacups."

Touching a lighted match to the tobacco, I draw on my briar and wink at Cal who watches the smoke trail off on the wind, just as she did as a child. My Callie girl—in on all these stories since she was a little tyke.

My cousins look miffed, but I don't care. Let 'em grumble. They sigh and fuss with their skirts, then settle back, finally ready to listen. They'll be all right. These benches are comfortable here in the shade. And I have plenty of sweet tobacco.

4

A Terrific Fever

I WAS ONLY SIXTEEN at the time, but I can recount every detail from the minute we got the telegram until the day we brought Amer back here to Rockford. But first, I want you to know about our uncle when he was alive.

Picture him loping across the yard toward our house—a square, two-story stucco farmhouse—waving his arms, clutching a fistful of brochures. That afternoon he'd ridden Bessie into Hadley, to the Engebretson Brothers' store and post office, and couldn't wait to show us what had arrived all the way from Saint Paul.

Amer had caught a terrific fever. Not the sick kind like scarlet fever, but the type that makes a fellow antsy. Lights up his eyes with possibilities. The kind of fever that sends a man westward.

At age thirty-eight, four years younger than my dad, he still looked like a boy. Slender with thin wrists hanging from the frayed cuffs of his blue chambray shirt—bleached pale from a hundred hot water washings. And eyes the color of that same shirt. His light brown hair looked like a big popcorn bowl had been plopped on top of his head, and somebody scissored off whatever stuck out below. Amer's face was tanned, except for his forehead, which was pale as winter wheat. We all looked like that during those prickly hot summer days in the fields.

Too old to go to war, my uncle seemed content to stay on with us, farming our rich southern Minnesota soil—good black loam. Till the fall of 1918. Then that Montana fever took over and nothing could bring it down. It all started with the set of broadsides he sent away for, dated September of that year. Within a few months, Amer would be leaving us, taking the first leg of his journey to the depot in Pipestone for that fateful "All aboard!"

The day those brochures arrived was like a smorgasbord. In place of food, a feast of possibilities. Mother had just finished washing up the dinner dishes and had gone upstairs to work on her mending. Dad was checking on the corn in a field behind our house. And Ray and I were tossing an old kittenball, playing keep-away with Sport and Docky, when Amer clip-clopped up the lane, urging Bessie along as fast as a workhorse can trot. He slid off her, scattering a klatch of squawking chickens on his way to the house, keeping pace with the dogs who joined in the race. Ray and I were right behind as Amer called over his shoulder, "C'mon, boys!" then took the steps three at a time and burst into the kitchen calling "Vic! Julia!"

Out of breath, he cleared the long table, moved the big sugar bowl, saltcellar, and jar of spoons to the cupboard. Scrubbed down the oilcloth. Rubbed it as if to erase its blue-checkered pattern. Then with a flourish, he spread his set of colored brochures from one end to the other, and with the sweep of an arm showed us what he was so excited about. What he'd been dreaming of for weeks: a land rush program in Eastern Montana, sponsored by the Chicago, Milwaukee and Saint Paul railroads, in connection with the Illinois Central and Great Northern transcontinental passenger trains. An invitation to heaven.

A farmer's paradise, proclaimed one folder, A land and wheat bonanza. Imagine getting in on that! As fast as the gandy dancers could pummel in those spikes, new lines snaked across open territory all the way to Seattle!

"Who's James J. Hill?" I asked Uncle Amer, noticing the name printed on each of the broadsides.

"A famous railroad tycoon," he said. "Offering free passage to lucky honyockers."

"What's a honyocker?" asked Ray.

"The opposite of a James J. Hill," he answered. "A poor sodbuster hoping to strike it rich."

Came to find out the term was a mean one. Derogatory. But Amer enjoyed saying it, always emphasizing the first syllable—HON-yocker—until the word floated around like any other and lost its meaning.

As if he were already on his way to broader horizons, Amer stepped in front of the kitchen window. Reading aloud from one of the pamphlets, he reached out as if to string his words across the treetops in the distant grove:

Come see the beautiful Yellowstone River, the booming town of Forsyth, and Custer County. Only three days by train and stage.

"Now what sort of fellow could resist that? he asked, leaning against the cook stove, arms crossed. "You've got this farm under control, Vic. And the boys have been working the fields and tending livestock like grown men for some time. I've just got to go out there and try my luck. If I don't catch hold of it now, I might never go."

Dad was quiet for a moment. "Well," he said in his drawn-out way, "we won't hold you back."

Uncle Amer's Adam's apple worked a few times before his wide grin overrode a brief look of apology.

From then on, he acted like one of us boys—Ray was sixteen and I was fifteen—fidgety and full of energy. Amer could hardly sleep at night. Sat up figuring out how much it would cost for seed, workhorses, field equipment, and drilling a well. In Eastern Montana, lumber was at a premium. He'd have to build a sod house.

"A sod house?" I asked. "What's that?

"Just what it sounds like," he answered.

In the early hours of a morning, if Ray or I had forgotten our chamber pot downstairs and had to go to the outhouse, we'd see a light beneath Amer's door. And hear the folding and unfolding of brochures and the eager scratching of pencil against paper.

So, of course, my brother and I caught the fever, too. We had never known anyone who'd traveled such a far distance on a train before. Well, there was Mrs. Gus Block. But she only went as far as Granite Falls, to take care of her dying sister.

Once, Ray and I each set a penny on the tracks to see what would happen when the wheels ran over them. We kept the flattened coins in little boxes in our dresser drawer. I say once, because Mother and Dad reminded us that we couldn't afford to throw money away like that.

Sometimes we walked "a tightrope" along the rails. Heel-to-toe, heel-to-toe. Faster and faster, skating up from behind to push the other off, trying to balance until one or both of us got tipsy and lost our footing. Took flight for a second, then tumbled and rolled over the stones and into the grassy ditch, laughing the whole time.

It seemed like a sort of graduation as we studied each broadside cover for ourselves. And imagined what it would be like riding inside one of those beautiful trains. Long trains curving around mountainsides and running alongside full rivers, pulled by powerful engines with cowcatchers on the front. Great black engines bound for glory.

I took up my new C-melody saxophone and tried to imitate the sound of those steel wheels rolling along the tracks. And that long, drawn-out whistle: Chooga-chugga, chooga-chugga, whoooa-whooo. What must the real thing sound like echoing through those canyons?

At breakfast the next morning, Amer laid out his plan. In detail. He would stake a 360-acre claim in Eastern Montana, north of Forsyth—somewhere between the little towns of Edwards and Jordan—and work the land until he could prove up on it.

"I'll be able to declare homestead within three years' time," he told us. Actually, he said it all many times. At breakfast, dinner, and supper. I suppose he thought the more often he told us of his plans, the quicker those three years would peel away from his calendar and he'd own the land.

"Why, I might even build me a fine ranch by then," he said, tapping the side of his head. "I already have the drawings up here."

Ray and I desperately wanted to go along. Seated across the table from Amer, we jiggled around in our chairs until you'd think we had the Saint Vitus Dance—so filled with the desire to pack our own bags. Even knowing how much we were needed at home, we argued and pleaded with Dad to let us go along.

Amer laughed at our boyish outbursts. And goaded us on, until Mother brought us up short with a scolding and painful tugs on our ears.

All Dad ever had to do to get us in line was fix us with his pale blue eyes and mutter, "Ip-ip-ip. You boys have to finish school. Amer will write and let us know all about the land."

"If the soil is as rich as James J. Hill says it is," said my uncle, "even half as good as what we have here, well...once I get my patent, you can come out for a visit. Who knows, you might even decide to stay on. I have a hunch there's going to be no place quite like Montana."

At some level, Amer must have known about the poor soil and drought conditions, the severe winters when prairie chickens and livestock froze to death, the demands of building a sod hut and managing livestock. But he was hooked on the idea of the place. Its possibilities. The beauty of it. You see, he was a Romantic. He quoted from Emerson to prove his point: "Life invests itself with inevitable conditions, which the unwise seek to dodge...." And, "All the good of nature is the soul's, and may be had if paid for in nature's lawful coin, that is, by labor which the heart and the head allow."

Although my uncle often talked about the facets of compensation from Emerson's essay, there was one line he never acknowledged, at least to us: "If the good is there, so is the evil."

Mother and Dad were happy for Amer, but I could tell they were worried. He was a strong, hard worker, but there was something different about him. Something not of the countryside. Whatever the chores—milking cows, manning a harrow, plowing up a garden for Mother's flowers and vegetables—he moved differently. Fluid-like, with a certain grace like those swans on Pine River, where Cal and I fished one summer.

He wasn't like the other farmers in the area. Especially those big Norwegians who seemed a little clumsy as they went about their lighter tasks. At the end of the day—once they'd finished the demanding, rhythmic picking of corn by hand, shocking hay, grubbing tree stumps, trudging along behind a plow and a team of workhorses through cloddy fields—those same farmers, toward dusk, moved like cripples across their yards. With buckets of oats and well water for the livestock gripped in gnarled hands, their gaits were pronounced by pained hitches, as if they had to will their backs and legs not to give out. Whereas Amer, light on his feet, seemed to dance through his evening chores.

The week before our uncle left, in March of 1919, Ray and I paid special attention to all of our "last times" together: the last time we ice-fished on Lake Summit where bands of Sioux Indians used to camp and where we found arrowheads in the spring; the last climb into our haymow to pitch feed down for the livestock; the last milk stream contest between Sport and Docky.

While we milked the cows, Amer had trained our Border collie and our Chesapeake hunting dog to stand opposite the dung trough, back of the stanchions. As soon as he shouted, "Ready, Set, Go!" the dogs—wild-eyed, jaws snapping, jowls flapping—lapped up the long, steamy squirts of milk we shot their way.

Some evenings, after chores, we put on musicales. Mother was always sending away for the latest sheet music from Minneapolis or Chicago: "Beautiful Dreamer," "Seated One Day at the Organ," "Mister Dunderback." She ordered songs from the great operas, too: Puccini's arias "Un Bel Di," "O Mio Babbino Caro," and "Nessun Dorma" from *Turandot*.

Oh, how we loved Puccini! Amer once said he wished he looked like him. And Mother thought he was just about the handsomest man she'd ever seen, besides Father. Mother and Amer played and sang those arias so often the rest of us couldn't help but repeat the Italian words, even if we didn't know what they meant.

Although none of us, except Amer, had quite the heart for it, we put on a regular gala the night before he left. Mother warbled and played accompaniment on our Chicago upright—that big old box of a piano. Dad kept time and danced around the parlor. Ray buzzed the tunes on a fine-toothed comb wrapped in tissue paper. And I played my C-melody, a saxophone I'd saved up for in order to form a high school dance band.

If walls ever stored such things, those making up our sturdy farmhouse would remember that music as long as they stood. Especially, Mother's flamboyant piano technique, Amer's beautiful tenor voice, and those plaintive notes from his violin.

His favorite tune (and ours) came from the opera *Gianni Schicchi*, just out in 1918. "Now there's a song," he used to say, "that would like to make you cry."

He couldn't seem to get the piece out of his head. And neither could we. He'd sing it while shaving or skipping down the steps for breakfast or balancing on a milking stool, one side of his face tight against a cow's warm flank, certain that the herd would give more milk if he gave them his music.

Amer sang loudest in the middle of a field, sounding like Enrico Caruso as he trudged along behind Fanny and Bessie: "*O mio babbino caro, mi piace è bello, bello.*" With rounded vowels and a haunting melody in ¾ time, that aria took hold deep inside us. We were careful, Ray and I, that no one should see how our eyes watered whenever we heard our uncle sing that song.

Oh, they sang for their supper that last night—Amer and his fiddle and Puccini.

5

All Aboard!

THAT FINAL MORNING came too soon for Ray and me. Excited and sorry at the same time, we hung around to watch Amer pack. He didn't have much: his Victrola and records, books, some clothing, and his beloved violin, a Farny with ivory inlay, wrapped in a clean feedsack.

In those days, Dad had an Overland Automobile, a 1914 model 79 Roadster, but it held only two people plus some stowage. So Ray and I hitched up the horses and loaded Amer's belongings onto the wagon, then hopped up and settled in next to the luggage, poking at each other in our excitement. Mother and Dad sat on the bench next to Amer, who drove the team. Holding the reins lightly, he guided Bessie and Fanny along the gravel road from our farm to

Hadley. We arrived at the depot just in time for Amer to purchase his ticket before we heard that awful and wonderful "All aboard!"

Amer was the only passenger leaving from Hadley station that day, on to Pipestone, then Granite Falls via The Great Northern. From there, Montana!

Never one to show his feelings, Dad simply shook hands with his brother and wished him well. Ray and I helped Amer with his luggage. He hugged Mother, shook hands with my brother and me, gave us each a little hug, then climbed aboard and walked down the aisle of the first car to an empty seat. From a lowered window, he flashed a smile that framed his straight, white teeth.

Dad stood next to the tracks, looking a bit downcast. Mother blew kisses, whipped her white handkerchief through the air, and sang out, "Promise to write!"

As the train inched away from the depot, Amer waved broadly from the open window. "You'll hear from me!"

With the rhythm of the engine, Ray and I danced and chanted, Amer's leaving, Amer's leaving—at first slowly, then faster and faster—Amer's leaving, Amer's leaving.... We jumped and waved and hollered till our socks sagged to our ankles and our voices fractured. Then, as the caboose made its turn past the willow trees and rolled out of sight— Amer's leaving Amer's leaving Amer's leaving—our voices trailed off.

And then he was gone.

We were all of us quiet as we returned to the horses and made our way back to the farm, hearing only the wagon wheels crunching against gravel, an occasional snort from Bessie or Fanny, a swish of a tail, and the rhythmic sounds of hooves.

Eventually, that long-awaited envelope arrived, post-marked Jordan, Montana, The Treasure State. That day, and from then on, whenever we received a letter from Amer, the four of us dropped whatever we were doing and gathered around the kitchen table while Mother read aloud.

From Fergus Falls to Valley City, North Dakota, the land begins to roll. The great Missouri River marked my passage and welcomed me into western country—Mandan and Custer land. The small buttes of western North Dakota grow massive near Miles City, Montana.

I imagined Amer taking in those sights from his train window, and tried to picture that exotic territory. Those changing land formations that really begin in North Dakota. I could just see Amer bursting with anticipation as he went over his list of needs for building a new life: equipment to purchase, land to work up for a first planting, a shelter to build, water to locate.

How many of those so-called "honyockers" felt uneasy

and had second thoughts about leaving the familiar in order to tackle the unknown, carrying only a few simple possessions and their life's savings? If Amer ever felt that way, he never let on. Jokes and music and a flurry of activity covered up any misgivings he might have had. His letters did the same. It was only later that we could read between the lines.

But those early letters contained the same optimism and sense of accomplishment Amer showed when we laid the corn by every summer—after that last round with the cultivator when the shoots have grown into thriving stalks tall enough to go it on their own. Corn borers and birds and other predators lived off some of the crop. We had to allow for that. But after our final round, it was simply a matter of waiting for the rest of it to grow up. And then harvest time.

*   *   *

"Oh," says Nellie, edging forward on her bench beneath the cottonwood branches, "I remember when the men laid our corn by. Once it was planted and cultivated, Daddy could finally find the time to drive us to Rockford to see a show."

Somewhat startled by Nellie's interjection, I nod in agreement and take a moment to relight my pipe.

"For us," I tell the ladies, "planting time was a regular celebration. Amer would spread his arms as if introducing those fledglings to the world. 'They're taking off on their own now, boys,' he'd say, 'so just sit back and watch 'em grow!'

"Ray and I would run to the pump house, plunge our arms up to the shoulders in that icy water and pull out bottles of Grape Nehi and Orange Crush and beers for Dad and Uncle Amer. Then we'd flop down on our bellies at the edge of a field and spy on the corn, certain we could detect a wobble in those yellow-green blades inching upward from the soil like tiny charmed snakes."

"And did they grow," asks Cal with a little smirk, "before your very eyes?"

"Certainly. If you had the patience to lie there long enough on a windless day and set your sights on a mark, why, yes, you could see it. Even when a shoot first broke through the soil, you could catch it dancing a slow waltz. Just a little thread bending toward the sunshine."

"Aw, Dad, is that true?"

"Could be. You have to have the patience for something like that."

"Yah, yah," says Hannah, "I've seen such a thing myself. Long ago, that is."

"Oh, I can just picture you," says Nellie, rolling her eyes. "There lies Hannah in the middle of a field, watching the corn grow."

"Yah, of course. Why not?"

"What would the neighbors say? Whatever would they

think?"

Hannah giggles. "They'd probably think I'd kicked the bucket."

"Yah, yah, toes turned up to the daisies."

"All right, Nell," says Hannah. "Let's get back to…"

"Or gone around the bend, on your way to the funny farm," Nellie persists.

"Yah, yah. That'll do, that'll do. Now let Willie get back to his story."

*   *   *

Amer's letters read like the chapters from a wonderful book. We could hardly wait for the next one to arrive.

Here's a line he wrote about Miles City. Don't you love the sound of that name? Miles City.

> *A bustling town in a valley surrounded by buttes colored with sunshine, shadows and a thousand shades of rose and ochre above sagebrush and laurel.*

This letter really tells what it was like for Amer:

> *I arrived in Forsyth, population 7,624, and stopped by the land office to sign the necessary papers and pay my filing fee of ten dollars. The acreage that I'll prove up in exchange for my labor is near a couple*

of little burgs called Edwards and Jordan, north of Forsyth. The buttes are gone with low mountains only in the distance.

It took some time and money lining up supplies. Some of the folks here are very critical of us "sodbusters." Many are helpful, but a few have had their fill of settlers flooding the land. And they let it be known. Too many families unprepared for what lay ahead.

I'm now the proud owner of a buckboard, four draft horses, some field equipment, and tools for building my sod house and digging a well. I might have to hire a drill. Some fellas told me they had to go down as far as two or three hundred feet to find water. I wonder if that's even possible.

I purchased a local history book at the General Store, so as to study up on this land I'll be calling "home." Had to laugh when the proprietor proffered his opinion about the great Missouri: "That river runs through two thirds the length of our state," he said, "too thick to drink, too thin to cultivate."

A couple of my horses are Belgian, said to be strong and tough. The other two are smaller and younger—part saddle horse, part Percheron. I can ride them, but they'll also be fit to help work the fields.

I purchased a good rifle and a Smith and Wesson .45, six shot and cartridges. I'm not at ease with a revolver, but one of the sodbusters I met up with said I should carry a sidearm. He said you never know what a man might come up against out here.

Imagine what I looked like sitting up high on a loaded wagon, giddyuppin' my team across the Forsyth-Yellowstone river bridge and onto the long open trail north as the crow flies, an endless brown ribbon cutting across the land. There's nothing like it back home.

Whenever I spot a stretch of long grass or wheat rolling with the wind, it reminds me of our big sloughs near Hadley and the waves on Lake Summit. I've never been on an ocean, but living out here in Eastern Montana might be the closest thing to it—a dry-land sea with plenty of elbowroom

Toward evening of the first day out, the sky turned deep violet, a backdrop for the livestock grazing in the distance: long wool sheep and cattle. The cattle were so still along the hillcrest and lower buttes, they seemed like cardboard cutouts against that sky.

I saw a lot of mule deer around the dried up creek beds, especially at dusk, but they skittered as soon as I drew near. They have large mule-like ears and *are brownish-gray in color with a white rump patch and a small black-tipped white tail.*

What unsettled me was the sight of so many animal carcasses. That tells you how rugged it is out here. I've never seen such vast country nor felt so alone. You should see the sky at night! It's huge and filled with the brightest stars I've ever seen.

By comparison, Minnesota seems closed in, as if a canopy were drawn over it. In this part of Montana, the sky is broader than you can imagine, and never-ending, just like the land. A three-quarter moon is nearly enough to read by. But when the sky is like pitch and there is no moon, the stars will do the job....

Amer took two days to cover the distance from Forsyth to Jordan, stopping off-trail where he could water and graze his horses and camp for the night. Several weeks went by before we heard from him again. And then he talked about his neighbors:

I have good neighbors. The McKammans are well established and live in a soddy across the road and down a quarter of a mile. They appear to be in their forties or fifties. I like to hear their Irish brogue. John is helping me get started, calls me "Swede." Mary frets about how thin I am. She bakes delicious

*pies whenever she can gather up a bowlful of berries
or a few apples. She sees that I eat my share.*

*A young shepherd dog found his way to my place.
I named him Radge. He's a fine one, makes for good
company. I call the horses Rounder and Sam, Johnny
and Skeeky. Does that ring a bell, Julia? They aren't
Bessie and Fanny, but they'll come around in due
time. I plan to buy a few head of cattle in a year
or so....*

*　　　*　　　*

"Goodness sake's alive!" says Hannah, standing up from
her bench to stretch. "His letters make that corner of the
world sound like heaven."

Nellie sniffs. "If it weren't for all those dead animals
along the way."

"I'll bet the hunting was terrific," says Cal. "Wonder if
there are any good fishing lakes around there."

"Some, but nothing like Minnesota. Although, he did
write about Fort Peck, a big lake connected to the Missouri
River, about twenty-five miles north of Jordan. He wanted to
go there, but it was too far and he couldn't spare the time."

I pick out another envelope from the small stack
next to me on the bench. "There are plenty of rivers, of
course, perfect for fly-fishing. I've only cast my line in lakes,
though."

"Me, too," says Cal, leveling an imaginary cast. She laughs when I ask her if she got a backlash.

"Our family news for Amer generally came from Mother's hand. Here's one of her notes:

Vic and the boys have been out hunting. They brought back three prairie chickens and I roasted them for supper last night. After chores on Saturday, Willie and Ray hiked to Lake Summit and caught a mess of bullheads. They wished you were with them. We miss you at the table and talk about how you always like your fish fried up nice and crispy. Can't you just smell them cooking?

We've had good weather; the corn and beans are coming along fine. Vic and the boys managed to seed some oats and put in a piece of flax. The neighbor's oats across the road are up—one of the first fields around. Willie got the garden tilled for planting the seeds we saved from last year.

We wonder how you are doing out there by yourself. Such hard work for one. And so far away. It isn't easy being separated from family. Wish I could have returned to Rockford just once before my mother and father passed on. Long distances are powerful hard. . . .

"Powerful hard," I repeat a little sadly. "You see, my mother, Julia, was just a young woman when she had to leave her parents and brothers and sisters behind in Rockford. Dad decided to move to Minnesota for the hunting and fishing shortly after Ray and I were born. For the first few years, while our farmhouse was being built, we lived in a timbered garage on that acreage north of Hadley. Mother never got over being uprooted, separated from her entire family. She cried a lot when my brother and I were little boys. Even when we grew older, we would sometimes catch her crying."

Quiet for a moment, I feel a sudden pang of loneliness for my mother, although she's been dead for nearly thirty years. I guess that feeling never goes away, no matter what.

"Yes, sir, makes no difference how old you are. Still seems like yesterday."

"How long has Vic been gone?" asks Hannah. "We drove up to Minnesota for his funeral. But it's been so long, I've forgotten the particulars."

"Thirty-four years. May the tenth, 1952."

"I was eight," says Cal. "I remember how hard it was to realize I'd never see Grandad again.

"What took him?" asks Nellie.

"Wrong type blood transfusion. But we could never prove it." I nod at Callie, remembering how it was for her. "He came through his operation just fine. Prostate surgery.

Didn't take him long to find his old self when we saw him in the recovery room. Mother walked over to his bedside and said, 'Vic, this is Julia. Do you recognize me, Vic? It's Julia.' At first, Dad pretended to be groggy. 'Julia?' he murmured. 'Julia?' Then he turned his head to squint at Mother. It was the grin that gave him away. 'Julia?' he said. 'I'd know your hide if it was tacked to the garage.'

Nellie frowns. Hannah laughs politely. Only Cal fully understands the affection behind those words.

"They lived at Lake Shetek back then," says Callie. "Tepeeotah."

"Yes, most evenings, you'd find Mother and Dad at the end of the pier, sitting side by each. But that wasn't going to happen again. You see, immediately after that blood transfusion, Dad took a turn for the worse. He was the last of the brothers to go."

"And Amer was the first," says Hannah.

"And our dads in between," adds Nellie. "No one knows what became of Uncle Reno."

"Probably faded away in some opium den in Chinatown," says Cal. "I've always been intrigued by what his life must have been like in San Francisco: craps, opium, brothels."

"I'd guess he was the complete opposite of Uncle Amer," says Nellie.

*   *   *

I sort through the envelopes lying next to me on the bench and continue with my story.

This next letter from Uncle Amer is a favorite of mine. Except for the last paragraph, which troubled the family and gave us the first indication that things weren't right.

April 20, 1919

Dear Family,

I suppose you're wondering what it's like out here. I get good advice from John and other "honyockers" who have worked through several seasons of crops. I'll put in winter wheat come September. For now I'll plant a little corn and some oats. Don't think I'll go for the sugar beets, although a few of the farmers are trying them. The big crop out here is wheat but there's concern about severe drought conditions affecting everyone and causing low yields. This yellowish soil doesn't seem as rich and giving as the black loam I'm used to.

Every day, I follow my team through the fields. We don't finish turning sod 'til evening and then we're plenty tired by the time we head for the corral. The "boys" are happy when I pull off their harnesses and cool them down with a good brushing. They earn their feed, that's for sure.

I don't change out of my work clothes until after I've cut a few "bricks" to add to my shelter. I had to learn how to build a soddy or 'dobe, as some call them out here. John helped me get started. I'm nearly finished, just need to rig up a window and locate a door. I've got my roof on—tarpaper over joists and topped with sod. Lumber is too expensive for more than the essentials, like ridgepole supports for the ceiling. I soak old newspapers and gather up mud and even a bit of horse dung for chinking holes. Mary had a few rags to spare for the purpose. Every bit helps to seal out the wind. So you see, I'm getting lined up for winter a little every day. I'm told it gets pretty cold in these parts.

My meals are mostly beef and boiled potatoes. Am eager to taste a few early vegetables. I'm getting along all right.

I don't keep up with washing my clothes like I should. I figure I'm going back into the fields come morning, so I hang my shirt and overalls on a nail in the door frame, ready to go. By now, they might stand up in a corner all by themselves. Oh well, it's clean dirt, I tell myself.

Before bed I wind up the Victrola and play along while night settles in. Seems like my songs get swallowed up out here. I like to watch the late-

working birds feed on what my plow turns over. It's as if they fly on the notes from my fiddle. Guess they approve. Radge runs his cuts and turns before settling down for the evening. You'd think he'd be tuckered out from following me around in the fields all day, but after supper he gets a fresh burst of energy and tries to herd the birds. You'd get a kick out of seeing him run free with a big grin on that long snout, stopping only to investigate a prairie dog hole.

I've met some good people, only there's one neighbor to the south by the name of Carmichael that's none too friendly. Doesn't seem to like my music. The other night I saw him ride his cow pony along the fence line that separates our land. He was looking out of sorts and whipping his horse's flank for no good reason that I could see. He gave me a stern look then charged away. Didn't think my notes were that sour! Guess I'll have to practice some more.

With the last paragraph of that letter began our concern about Amer's safety. One of those uneasy feelings you try to shake off but can't. The following afternoon, he would give Tom Carmichael wide berth when he met up with him in

Jordan. The court records included this testimonial from a witness:

> Amer Lindstrom had just stepped onto the boardwalk in front of the post office when the confrontation took place. Tom Carmichael and his brothers, Jim and Seth, came on like schoolyard bullies and fanned out in front of Mr. Lindstrom. Tom sneered and said, "Boys, I see a lily-liver comin' our way. What are we gonna do about that?" Mr. Lindstrom met their glances with his hands at his sides. He is a peaceful man from what I know of him. The Carmichaels, all large men, crowded and elbowed him off the boardwalk and onto the street. Then Tom pushed him down. I heard him tell Mr. Lindstrom that he had better watch his back because there'd be "a next time."

This witness, a Mr. Johanssen, goes on to say there was no mistaking Tom Carmichael because of an unusual laugh that started deep in his throat and rose to a snarl. He had a penchant for shooting dogs roaming around the outskirts of town and picking fights with honyockers, especially those who didn't blend in with the locals or the first wave of settlers. They were a tough bunch, those Carmichaels, a trio of bullies.

*　　*　　*

I get up from my bench to show the ladies a small black-and-white snapshot of Amer in front of his soddy, with Radge by his side.

"Oh my," says Hannah, "look how his clothes hang. He must have lost a lot of weight."

Nellie leans over for a peek. "Is that his place? Why, those little buildings rise up so tiny against the sky. And such wide open land." She shivers. "It looks awful lonely out there."

"But see the way Amer stands," says Cal, "with his feet planted wide and his shoulders back? He's waving—waving his hat at the sky."

"I've always liked this picture," I murmur, studying it for a moment before tucking it back into its envelope. "Hell, he looks as if he owns Montana."

"Well, he looks dirt poor to me." Nellie crosses her arms. "And starving."

"Like nearly everyone back then, Amer was most likely broke, having spent all his savings on getting started, equipment and horses. And he never asked for help. In all that time, he never asked but for one thing and I'll get to that in a minute. First, I want to read from his next letter, which, I'm sorry to say, contains the last of his true optimism:

May 22, 1919

As busy as I am, these three years should sail by before my patent comes through. The work is hard but my horses and I make up a good team by now, almost come full circle after the spring planting and cultivating. They say the summers don't last long out here. I'm eager to put in my winter wheat. In past years, some of the farmers got as much as twenty-five bushels per acre. Isn't that something? We could use a little rain. No, a <u>lot</u> of rain. It doesn't look promising, but they say it'll come. They're hoping for the same bumper yields as between 1910–17. The war pushed the price up to $2.00 a bushel. It might even double. Imagine that!

I rigged a fifty-gallon drum inside my soddy to burn kerosene when it gets cold. The railroad sells coal but it's too costly for my pocket. I use hay and swampgrass twisted into what they call "cats." That way it burns longer.

And I fixed up a shelf for my books out of scrap wood left over from the roof wedges. Radge and the horses will keep me company when the blizzards hit. Otherwise, I'll try to get over to the McKammans' now and again.

"See what I mean? Doesn't that sound hopeful? But the thing is, after the altercation in town, the Carmichaels grew uglier, bored with their petty threats. When they couldn't get a rise out of Amer, they likely figured there was no way he'd give up and abandon his land. And that's when they came calling."

6

The Hundred Dollar Smile

IT WAS NO SOCIAL CALL. Those Carmichael brothers
—they were bad eggs.

I was struck by how Amer reported the attack, how he
wrote it up in such detail. His affidavit reminded me of a
script for a scene in some macabre play. Actually, the word
"affidavit" sounds too formal when I think of those large,
yellowed sheets of paper—a document written in Amer's
hand with the same brown ink and curlicues as on his letters
home to us. That original document had been attached to a
typed version, filed in the sheriff's office, and used as evidence
during the trial. Because of Amer's detailed testimony and
what the McKammans told us about the night of July 14,
1919, I felt as if I'd been there. Witnessed the whole thing.

Yet unable to ward it off.

Amer had just finished feeding Radge when the three Carmichaels—Tom, Seth, and Jim—rode up to the common gate on horseback. Amer might have gone along with Tom saying they just wanted to talk to him. But when one of the men made a belittling remark about extending an invitation for tea, Amer warned them not to come any further. To stay off his land, period. The Carmichaels laughed and jeered, then charged in through the open gate and immediately surrounded him. They rode around Amer in a tight circle, telling him the land wasn't his and never would be, that this was no place for the likes of him, and he should wise up and go back home where he belonged. Back to that milquetoast state of Minnesota.

Amer edged toward his rifle, which was propped against the soddy, but all three men slid off their horses and closed in on him before he could get to it. For some reason, he didn't have his revolver. The McKammans told us later on that he never wore it.

"This little guy needs some encouragin'," Seth said, throwing a quick punch at Amer's face as if to tease him. Amer ducked and raised his fists in self-defense, but Jim and Seth grabbed him and pinned his arms. Tom doubled him over with a punch to the midsection, then snapped his head back with a knee to the jaw. He spat on him and snarled,

"If you knew what was good for ya, you'd pack up your

fiddle and clear out! Your kind ain't welcome here."

And he whacked him so hard with the butt of his pistol that Amer's teeth caved in like a handful of pebbles. Jim and Seth dropped him and he crumpled to the ground, bleeding from his mouth and nose. They'd broken his jaw and ruptured blood vessels around his stomach. Barking in a frenzy, Radge lunged at the men. Before Amer passed out, he heard an awful yelp and caught sight of his dog flipping head over tail off Seth's boot.

It was dark when Amer came to. He lay on the ground for some time, then crawled inside his shelter and managed to wet a cloth for the swelling on his face. He heaved enough blood and tooth fragments to line the washbasin. Radge limped in and collapsed next to the bed. Amer was glad to see him alive. If the Carmichaels hadn't already knocked the dog senseless, they might have shot him. Tom was most likely playing it smart so as not to attract the neighbors with the sound of a gunshot, especially from a revolver.

The following morning, John McKamman broke from work to check on Amer, concerned when he didn't see him in his field; he was usually the first one out. Shocked by the bloody mess, he quickly bound the dog's ribcage, at Amer's insistence, then rushed my uncle into town to see the doctor and to file charges with the sheriff.

How we wished it had all stopped there. And that he could have received the protection he needed and deserved.

I believe the law let him down.

This next letter, dated July 18, 1919, is the one that alarmed us—even though, as we learned later, it underplayed what really happened:

> *Now I don't want you to worry but some fellas got into a fight with me and beat me up pretty bad. They knocked out a big share of my teeth and I don't have the money for dentures and could use a little help. Once I get fixed up and put things to right on my place, I'll come back for a visit. I'm eager to see you and the folks in Hadley town. And the farm!*
>
> *By the way, how's the corn? Suppose you laid it by some weeks ago. Be sure to keep an eye on it, boys!*
>
> *I'll be all right. This business with my teeth and jaw set me back from getting at my work. I won't be scared off, though, from seeing my homestead title made official.*
>
> *I sure miss all of you.*

We hoped Amer would come back Johnny-on-the-spot to Minnesota. Mother and Dad rushed over to the bank in Hadley to borrow some money, which they wired to Uncle Amer, including a little extra for train fare and a telegram urging him to be wary and to come home without delay.

At the time, we didn't know any details about what had brought on this attack. No idea who these people were or what they might do next. Was the law watching out for Amer? It didn't seem so. We were terribly anxious to hear from him again. And so relieved when he sent this next letter, thanking us, grateful to begin the process of getting fitted for false teeth. That's when he finally admitted what was going on:

> These fellas to the south, the Carmichael brothers, think I'm an easy target. They're trying every way they can to jump my claim and scare me off the land. I'm determined to hold on until my homestead papers come through. The headaches are pretty bad from the broken bones around my jaw and teeth. Hard to eat, keep up the strength I need for my fieldwork.
>
> I notified the sheriff as to what happened. Not sure what more they can or will do, the sheriff and his deputy.
>
> I'm eager to see you. And boys, you'd better get out there and dig some worms and rig up the fishing poles so we can catch a mess of fish at Lake Summit.
>
> Meet me at the station in Pipestone. I'll be the man with the hundred-dollar smile!

Oh, boy, were we happy! Excited? We could hardly wait! Mother and Dad planned a big hoopla—wrote invitations, bought party favors, lined up our music, decorated the parlor with colored paper chains and stitched together a WELCOME HOME! banner that we draped along the wall above the piano. Mother even ordered a packaged assortment of balloons, "dye guaranteed not to rub off." It would be like welcoming Amer back from some foreign country, from the war, even.

Our kitchen smelled wonderful from all the food we were preparing: baked bread and mounded pies filled with slices of apples from last year's crop, roasting chickens and roast beef and pork. While Mother dressed out the game birds, Ray and I shelled peas and snapped the tips off string beans. Dad strung the last of our paper streamers above the dining room table.

In the middle of all this, there came a knock at the door. I jumped up to answer it, expecting to see a neighbor or Gus Block from the Hadley Co-operative stopping by with extra butter. Instead, it was Mr. Byers, the wireless operator from town. He stepped inside the entry and stood for a long moment, somber, reluctant to hand over the thin half sheet of pale yellow paper he'd drawn from his satchel. Across the top, in bold type, were the words Western Union.

I felt the joyful energy of party preparations drain from my entire body. Legs and arms and hands felt numb, went limp as my mind raced to consider Mr. Byers' demeanor and what possible message that little piece of paper could contain. A clammy knot centered in my midsection, as if I'd just been punched. I called for Dad.

The three of us stood too close together in our narrow entry: Mr. Byers' back tight against the screen door; Dad and I facing that tiny piece of paper as if it were a firing squad. No one had to read the words. By the grim expression on Mr. Byers' face, we knew. There's a strange ambivalence that sets in when you're confronted with such a thing: You don't want to know. And at the same time, you need to know for certain what you already know.

With reluctance, my dad reached out and took it. Mr. Byers let go of the flimsy sheet and slowly turned toward the door. "I'll wait outside for your reply, Vic," he said in a dull voice.

At times like that, everything alternately races and shifts to slow motion and you become aware of the minutest things: a dirt smudge on the entry wall; your father's work-worn fingers pinching the edge of a telegram, letting it hang at his side, reluctant to look at it; his bent back and sluggish movements as he manages the five steps up to the kitchen.

Now, seventy years later, I can remember my own quick breaths and my father standing in the middle of our farmhouse kitchen, surrounded by colorful party favors and all that wonderful food, reading three short lines on a

Western Union telegram—silently at first. Then he looked up with the most wounded eyes I've ever seen on a man. Stricken physically, as if he had just taken an awful lashing, he read in a thin, raspy voice,

This is to notify you Amer Lindstrom shot and killed near Jordan Montana stop burial in local cemetery if body not claimed within three days stop please advise stop

Bart Fleming, the sheriff of Garfield County, had signed the telegram.

Mother and Ray froze where they stood, dumbfounded. Although I'd already had a bit of time to register its probable contents, the words on that little piece of paper hit me like an axe against a chopping block. Hard to fathom, when one minute you're in the middle of plans for a reunion party and the next.... Dad said nothing more for the longest time. He lowered his arm and let the yellow paper hang by his side while he gripped the edge of our cook stove, his face drained of color, his jaw set. He stared out of the window in the direction of the barn and the distant grove, sucking in quick, heavy breaths through his nose. That kitchen was so quiet you could hear the rhythmic whistling of Dad's breathing. Mother collapsed onto a chair and lifted her apron to her face. Ray began to cry. I felt like throwing up.

Since Amer's last letters, we'd had a bad feeling about "that Godforsaken country," as Mother called it. But this....

After a lengthy silence, Dad turned away from the window, laid the telegram on the table, cleared his throat, and spoke in a strained, yet determined, voice: "I won't have my brother buried like a pauper," he said. "Unmarked and forgotten. We're bringing him home to Rockford."

From the hutch drawer he took a tablet and a pencil and sat down to write. Ray and I moved aimlessly about the kitchen. When Dad finished, he got up and headed for the door. I followed him down the steps and outside where he thanked Mr. Byers and handed him our reply:

arrival within three days stop please hold body at undertaking parlor stop   Victor Lindstrom

Mr. Byers, who knew and respected Amer, read the message, then paused, searching for his own words. He shook his head and placed his hand on Dad's shoulder.

"I'm sure sorry, Vic." Then he turned to me and said, "I'm awfully sorry, son. I know that Amer was like another father to you boys."

As far as I'm concerned, now that I'm an old man, the hardest thing a person has to do in life is turn his back on one who has just died. Turn his back and walk away. Take care of the necessaries.

Almost as difficult is re-entering a house that shouts merriment and celebration when fate has played a mean trick, pulled the ace of spades from its sleeve, and there's nothing left to celebrate. As I've said before, it's at times like that when you notice the littlest things: a smooth gray pebble on the ground, crossed blades of quack grass at the edge of a path, a tuft of dog fur caught in the wire gate, the veins in a single maple leaf, oblivious chickens bustling about the farmyard, Fanny whinnying in the pasture. Then there was Bessie, resting her muzzle on the wooden fence, standing very still with a quizzical look, watching us plod up the steps to our door as if she sensed something amiss. You see, she was Amer's favorite.

Inside our house, Ray scurried through the rooms like a little kid, tearing down paper streamers and bursting the balloons. He stomped on those that didn't break between his fingers. No one stopped him. Afterward, he crumpled to the floor, next to the piano.

Mother let the fire burn out in her cook stove and placed the meat and wild game in the icebox. I cleared the table and stacked the good dishes on the top shelf of the hutch. My father left the kitchen with telegram in hand. Gripping the long banister, he inched up the stairs like an invalid.

Later that evening, as the four of us sat around the supper table, eating very little, Dad announced his plan. I suddenly felt older than my sixteen years when he told me that I was to go out west with him to claim the body.

"We'll leave first thing in the morning," he said. "And Ray, you're to stay with Mother. Tend the farm while we're gone."

My brother looked stunned. "Why? Why does Will get to go?"

No one spoke.

"I'm older than he is! I'm the one should go with you!"

"It's decided," Dad said in a quiet voice.

Ray slid his chair back from the table and jumped up, knocking over a glass of milk. He ran to the door, yanked it open, and slammed it on his way out.

Mother got up to follow him.

"Let the boy be," said Dad, reaching for her hand. "He'll have to work through it on his own."

Mother did not sit down again. Instead, she stood at the window, watching, waiting. Then she dipped a washrag into a pan of water, wrung it out, and began wiping down the cook stove, all the while glancing out of the window.

Without being told, I knew why Dad had picked me to go with him to Montana. I felt proud, grown up, yet sorry for my brother. After that night, Ray and I were never again the same towards one another. From then on, we would pay a big price for Dad's decision, even though it was the right one.

7

Indelible Mark

RAY SLEPT IN THE BARN that night and only returned to the house for breakfast the next morning. Mother tiptoed out with a blanket and pillow, while Dad and I pored over the same railroad maps and timetables and brochures that Amer had sent away for, then left on the bureau in his old upstairs bedroom. "I won't need these any longer," he'd said. "I'll soon be living the dream."

For me, the pictures of the Illinois Central and Great Northern had not only lost their luster, they seemed downright foreboding. The vegetation around the mountainside was brown and dry. And that charging black engine fronted with a cowcatcher looked especially threatening, like a weapon, like an outrageous barrel on some strange, gigantic shotgun.

The next morning, we drove directly to the train station in Pipestone and bought passage on The Great Northern, just as Amer had done months earlier. Like mourners next to an open grave, Mother and Ray stood at the edge of the platform several feet above the tracks, awaiting our departure.

As the train surged away from the terminal, I leaned out of an open window to look back at the other half of my family, wondering if I'd ever see them again. What were we getting into? Would we make it back alive? Mother blew a kiss and waved a handkerchief with her fingertips, as if she were shaking dust from it. Ray stood next to her, eyes downcast, fists jammed deep into his pockets. I realized then that my brother would never get the chance to say goodbye to Amer, never see him one last time. He and Mother would have to stay back to oversee the farm and tend the livestock while Dad and I took the six-day journey into the unknown and back again—a bitter adventure that would leave an indelible mark on my brother and me for the rest of our lives.

As the hours passed, jostled in our seats by the monotonous movement of the train, I tried to read my dad and look to him for a little comfort. But there was none. From the blank look in his eyes to the little muscles around his mouth, I could detect no sign of emotion. After his initial reaction to the telegram, he simply went into himself—his thoughts locked away, his face immoveable as stone. I sat back and let myself be lulled by the swaying motion and rhythmic clickety-clack of the wheels. From my window, I mindlessly watched the comings and goings of green fields, pastures, fence lines, horses and cattle, a few sheep, shady groves, an occasional lake or slough. As the train slowed for crossings, it became easier to track the even rows of soybeans and tall corn. After a while the hypnotic rhythm of the rails and the purpose of our journey planted new words in my mind: *Amer's waiting, Amer's waiting, Amer's waiting . . . .*

We stayed the first night in Granite Falls, then traveled for two more days and nights. At Miles City, we had to board the branch train to Forsyth. Dad had said next to nothing during the entire trip, except for a few passing comments in the dining car or in the sleeping car while dressing for bed. Each night, he honed his straight razor on the wide leather strop he'd brought along. Having been a barber in Rockford before moving to Hadley, he was meticulous and ritualistic, making sure his razor was sharpened for his next morning's shave. I'd sit on the top bunk in my pajamas, legs dangling over the edge, and think up things to say. I guess I talked enough for both of us. About Amer and his land, about the men who had beaten, then murdered him. I created a dozen different scenarios for how he might have avoided getting killed:

"He should've practiced using his revolver and worn it in a holster at all times.

"He should have pressed charges after he was beaten up and insisted that the sheriff throw Tom Carmichael in jail.

"He should've gunned down those dirty varmints the minute they surrounded him, before they could lay a hand on him."

"He should have…"

Finally, Dad said, "Try to rest, son. We're going to need our strength and our wits when we get to Jordan."

After running out of words, I tricked myself into thinking that maybe, just maybe, there'd been a mistake. Someone else had been killed: a case of mistaken identity. Things like that happened all the time. Wouldn't it be something if my uncle were still alive? By golly, he'd be all right! He'll meet us at the station. Yes, by God, he'll be there to take us out to his land and show us the soddy he'd built and the fields he's going to plant in wheat. Dad and I will settle in, unpack, figure out where we'll sleep; Amer will have brought in a couple of extra cots for us. Or bedrolls on the floor. Or we could sleep outside, next to a campfire. Then we'll fuss over Sam and Rounder, Johnny and Skeeky, and brush and feed and water them. And Radge—I can't wait to run with that dog while he scares up birds. We'll all have a good laugh as soon as we see that wide grin at the end of Radge's snout.

"Good night, Will," said Dad, snapping my fantasy out of existence. "Morning comes early."

During the last part of our journey, I whiled away the

hours continuing to stare out the window, taking in the landscape as Amer must have seen it: the sun focusing on remarkable stone outcroppings, striking the faces of buttes, giving off shades of rose and mauve and ochre. Banks of aspen and pines growing up from the valley, defining crevices and the twists and turns of the river.

The Yellowstone flows along the edge of town, in the opposite direction from where we were going. But the river wasn't as full and rushing as I thought it would be. In some places it presented itself as little more than a trickling creek. Then I remembered having heard about the terrible drought. As soon as we arrived in Forsyth, I saw just how low and yellow the water was, stained by the soil.

It was midmorning of the third day when our train pulled into the Northern Pacific & Milwaukee terminal in Forsyth, Montana, an up-and-coming town with some of the most impressive houses and Main Street edifices I'd ever seen. I especially liked the Rosebud County Courthouse. Much later, I would learn that it had been built in 1914, just five years before Dad and I made that trip. Twelve years after Rosebud was created from the western half of Custer County. It has always amazed me what human beings are capable of building once they set their minds to it: that courthouse, for instance, with its huge portico and octagonal tower topped by a copper dome.

His voice hinting at irony, Dad called it "The Glory of

Forsyth."

And to think that not all that many years later, I would have an office inside "The Glory of Masterton," our Maywood County Courthouse, every bit as stately, with its own arched entry and bound ledgers (some dating back to 1887) tucked away in our office vaults.

Dad and I collected our bags and stepped down onto the platform, uncertain what to do next or where to find transportation to Jordan. The air was warm and dry. Some passengers set down their luggage on the dusty ground and rushed with open arms toward close friends or family. Others moved about deliberately, a few of the men stopping to check the time on their chained pocket watches.

"How will we get there?" I asked, feeling apprehensive.

Dad looked around for a minute, then pointed off to the side, beyond the depot. "I believe that fellow's for hire," he said, leading the way towards a man in a long brown duster and tan driving cap, standing next to an impressive-looking vehicle.

I stopped in my tracks when I spotted that fancy contraption: a four-door horseless carriage, mustard-colored, with seats in front, a bench behind, a space for luggage, and a third row of seats. Two spare tires were strapped to the rear. I'd never seen a car like it.

Dad rubbed a hand across his clean-shaven face. "I believe they call it a stage," he said.

"It doesn't look like any of the stagecoaches I've seen in the movies."

"Course not," he answered. "I saw one once in a picture —some of our war generals riding in a car like that."

Dad approached the owner and shook hands with him. "That's quite a vehicle," he said.

Mr. Malloy, standing at attention, told us that he was for hire and suggested we leave for Jordan after taking our noon meal. But when Dad explained the urgency of our trip and what had happened to Uncle Amer, he agreed to start out immediately. We assured him that we'd eaten a filling breakfast on the train and were eager to get going. He and Dad settled on the price of a dollar a day.

I was relieved to meet the likes of Mr. Malloy, a man with a rough edge, but compassionate. And familiar with the territory. At age sixteen, this was my first experience away from the farm. And being out in an uncertain world. Finding an ally, someone who'll stick by you in tough times, makes all the difference. I hoped Mr. Malloy would be able to help us from beginning to end—out of Forsyth to Jordan and back again. And that nothing bad would happen to any of us.

While Mr. Malloy filled several canteens with fresh water from a fountain near the train station, Dad and I admired the car, a seven-passenger motorized Cadillac. It had been turned into the kind of vehicle that, free of dust, might have opened its doors to a passenger dressed in tuxedo pants, a smoking jacket, and spats. Or to a general in uniform. Mr. Malloy never slouched while standing next to it.

We stowed our luggage in a space beneath the rolled up canvas that was used as a convertible top during inclement weather. Our driver got in and pumped up the fuel pressure by pushing and pulling on a rod to the right of the steering wheel. He turned the key to start the engine, adjusted the choke, and off we went in grand style—in an open touring car, just like General Pershing.

Because the day was hot and dry, we were able to cover the one hundred miles to Jordan under a clear sky. And because we were the only passengers, we rode up front with Mr. Malloy, who sat ramrod straight behind the wheel.

As we motored through the main streets of Forsyth, he pointed out the Choisser Block, a wholesale liquor emporium, the Alexander Hotel, and the Forsyth Meat Market, housed in what used to be the Merchant's Bank. Seeing the long links of sausages draped in the window made me hungry. After the courthouse, my favorite building was the Commercial Hotel, decorated in a diamond pattern with light and dark bricks made in the brickyard south of town. I was so taken with Forsyth and Mr. Malloy's narration that, for a minute, I almost forgot why we'd come to Montana.

Then a vision of Amer waiting for us at the undertaking parlor in Jordan hit me hard. If only my uncle had changed his mind and stayed in Forsyth. Yet, I couldn't imagine him working in a store or sitting behind a desk in some office. He was too much of a romantic for that. He was a homesteader.

The modern appearance of the bridge that would take us out of town surprised me. I had envisioned a rickety old wooden span, much like a railroad trestle. Mr. Malloy called the structure a "pin-connected through-truss bridge," explaining that the concrete piers and steel components had been fabricated in Pennsylvania, shipped by rail, then assembled and dedicated in 1905. "Hundreds of people," he boasted, "came to that dedication." Before the new bridge was erected, he said, Rosebud County residents had to ford the Yellowstone in low water, depend on irregular ferry service in high water, or travel forty-five miles downstream to Miles City in order to get to the other side.

Inevitably, at frequent moments in our conversations, sadness and guilt came down over me like a heavy curtain, ending my brief enthusiasm for a bit of history, a beautiful building, a pretty girl walking down Main Street. We hadn't come to Montana for the sights. Although, it was pleasant to remember what Uncle Amer had written in one of his letters about the river and how it got its name: the Minnetaree Indians, first settlers, called it the Yellow Rock River. French trappers named it *Roche Jaune*, translated to Yellowstone by Lewis & Clark. *Roche* means rock, Amer contended, so why not call it that? Yellow Rock River.

And so, Mr. Malloy drove us across the through-truss bridge, leaving Forsyth and the low level of the Yellowstone behind. Thus began the final leg of our journey over the land of the Minnetaree, on the same dirt trail Amer had traveled months earlier.

8

That Montana Sky

I THOUGHT SO HARD ABOUT my uncle during our passage from Forsyth to Jordan that I could picture him on the horizon, at the top of each little hillcrest. A lone man on a buckboard heaped with supplies, guiding four big horses into what would turn out to be called The Badlands of Eastern Montana. I strained to hold him in my vision, until I could have sworn he was there, just ahead of us, and we would soon catch up with him. But it was only a mirage. And mirages, as everyone knows, are things you can never close in on.

With few intersections, the trail stretched as far as you could see and then some. In his letters, Amer called that road "a long brown ribbon, turned black after dark." It was a difficult trail, bumpy and full of deep ruts. A few times I thought we'd rip out an axle. The ride was made bumpier by the wheels—no such thing as inflatable rubber tires—and it made my young bones ache. It was to be a long trip. Night would fall before we reached Jordan.

Just then a wolf howled in the distance.

"A wolf cry at midday," said our driver, shaking his head. "Bad omen."

I shivered and glanced sideways at Mr. Malloy, waiting for him to explain. But he said nothing more and kept his eyes on the trail.

Besides his duster and hat, he wore leather driving gloves and goggles with barely a trace of dust on them. He was a good-natured sort with a ready smile, an abrupt manner, watchful brown eyes, and a sidearm. Guess you had to be tough to live out west, though he showed a different side when it came to his vehicle. Easing around potholes, he called her "My Jenny." Gave her little pats on the dashboard whenever the machine got us through a particularly rough section of road. During our rest stops, he wiped off the grime with one of several rags and checked under the hood to see if she needed a drink or a little oil. He kept containers of gasoline, water, and oil on the floor of the third seat and repeatedly checked on those two spare tires lashed to the rear end.

"Taking proper care of my Jenny," he said, "can make the difference between life and death in this part of the country."

I didn't doubt him. Throughout the day, we never saw another soul on that dusty trail.

"A wolf howling at midday, Mr. Malloy," I said. "Why is that a bad omen?"

"Signals a predicament. Wolves generally talk to each other early in the morning and at night. This one might mean a long separation from its pack or a fight over territory."

"Has any animal ever tried to chase you down?" asked Dad. "Making this trip?"

"Oh, no," he said, patting the dashboard again. "My Jenny here gets us through these crossings without so much as a nip at her hindquarters."

He laughed and sat up even straighter than before.

Mr. Malloy came to life whenever he talked about having such a modern conveyance for traveling across those great stretches of land. Dad had been right: that stage was the same model as those the government shipped to Europe for the war in 1917, used for staff cars and ambulances. In fact, Mr. Malloy's car had been in France during that time. Had a bullet hole shot through the hood on the driver's side, next to the latch. It angled down steeply to the floor where a secondary hole had been patched. Mr. Malloy figured it had likely happened at the second or third Battle of the Marne, either from the air or by a shooter taking a bead on the driver. He'd left the outside bullet hole as a reminder of the Great War, but had painted over the olive-drab body until it acquired a mustard tint.

The year before, on November 11, 1918, my friends and I had skipped school so we could march in an impromptu Armistice Day parade. I was fifteen years old. What a coincidence that the very next year, I would imagine myself in a half-crouch on the running board of Mr. Malloy's touring car, gun in hand, peering over my shoulder while our driver outran the Germans.

"General 'Black Jack' Pershing was very happy with his Cadillacs," explained Mr. Malloy. "They were fully armored with Colt machine guns for the fight against Pancho Villa, in the border war with Mexico. Many of the cars broke down, having no interchangeable parts. Even so, it was quite an advancement. You see it was the first time in history that the United States fought a ground war using mechanized vehicles in place of horses and mules."

Wide-eyed and feeling patriotic, I might have enlisted right then and there in the middle of Montana's Badlands. I saw myself tearing down to Mexico in that Cadillac rigged with machine guns in search of Pancho Villa and his men.

"What else, Mr. Malloy?" I asked, eager for more, glad

to be thinking other thoughts for the time being. "Why did they choose cars like this one?"

"General Pershing had a hunch, helped convince the government to run tests on them for two thousand miles across the Chihuahuan Desert, near Marfa, Texas. I'm pleased to report that not only did the touring car finish the test, it continued for another five thousand miles."

"Wow!" I said. "Imagine that! Five thousand miles!"

"And that was in the heat of July 1917," said Mr. Malloy. "Turned out they only needed a thirty-cent fan spring and a gallon and a half of water."

"With that kind of record," said Dad, "I can see why they'd use them for the war effort."

Mr. Malloy wiped a tiny spot of grease off the steering wheel with his handkerchief. "Yep. Our government wasted no time shipping a fleet of these cars to France. Have no fear. She'll get you to Jordan and back."

Practically by the book, our driver knew everything there was to know about his 'Jenny' and her relatives. I looked at Dad, seated to my right. His expression reminded me of a picture I'd seen of General Pershing in 1914, looking at once stern and sad. The General had just lost his wife and three daughters in a fire at the Presidio in San Francisco. Only his little boy survived. How could anyone go on living after something like that?

For the little boy, I guess.

There we were in that big car with a flag holder soldered to the front and an unmistakable bullet hole in the hood, on our way to retrieve Uncle Amer's body, as if he'd been killed in the war. Except his was a little war—a war over a land claim. Or had Tom Carmichael murdered him for a different reason? Why would anyone kill another person over a piece of land? Especially when it wasn't all that productive. But that was war for you.

"Here in the West," continued Mr. Malloy, "these cars are, of course, far more comfortable than the old Concorde stagecoaches and six-horse teams from the 1800s. Those had to stop every ten miles or so, next to Little Porcupine Creek and Little Dry Creek, where there was some water and grass for the horses and food for the passengers. Though you had to be careful where you stopped in those days."

He'd heard of a woman by the name of Mrs. Corbet who planted herself in the middle of the trail, pointed her gun at the driver, and demanded that he pull over. Then she forced the passengers to eat a meal at her table for one dollar per without any comment. That's how he put it, "one dollar per without any comment." He didn't know if she ever shot anyone, but heard she got to be very rich.

"Oh, Amer would sure get a kick out of that story," I said, imagining how exciting it would be to meet such folks along the way. As long as they didn't kill you.

Eventually, we did encounter one such at the halfway

point—a grizzly old guy in filthy clothes, with sunken gray cheeks and a wary eye. A yellow-gray beard hung over the bib of his crusty overalls. Those whiskers were as matted and full of crud as unwashed fleece, a wood tick hideout.

Packs of skinny dogs roamed around outside the shack. The old guy never got up from his chair, a sturdy contraption made from thick branches and sticks bent into shape and nailed together. He sat tilted back against a wall in the shade of an overhang, clutching a revolver on one knee and a bottle of whiskey on the other. I figure that whiskey is all he ever swallowed, because you couldn't drink the water, bitter as it was, tainted with alkali. Mr. Malloy warned us about that— a salty mineral that seeps through the soil and into the water. It smells bad, too, as if other stuff has seeped into it. Anyhow, the three of us drank soda pop fished from a large cooling box that hadn't seen ice in a long time. The inside was grimy with dirt and dried rodent carcasses and we had to wipe coats of dust off the bottles before opening them.

You'd have thought the old man would be eager for company, but he never budged, except to set down his whiskey bottle so he could hold out a hand for our money. Never did hear the sound of his voice. Wonder if he even had one?

We decided to wait for other toilet facilities…a stop along the trail, because the pit behind that old guy's shack was so foul you couldn't get within ten feet of it without gagging. I was glad to get out of there and back into our car.

It took a good mile in the open air before that stench cleared from my olfactories. To this day, I can conjure up those awful smells (not that I care to) and that place, which comes to me in shades of tanned leather and dried cornstalks. In my mind that old geezer sits propped against a splintered wall, swilling his brew, gun at the ready, until such time as he drops over dead. For all I know he and his dogs are still there, gone to dust and skeletons next to the remnants of that old stick chair. Nothing left but empty whiskey bottles, a gun, and piles of bones.

"I've been by there any number of times," said Mr. Malloy, "and the old codger never shows the slightest indication that he recognizes me. Ekes out a living the only way he knows how. Probably started out kinda hopeful, just like those sodbusters who thought the land would provide as soon as it went under the plow. And the weather would behave itself. Problem was they weren't only farmers from your neck of the woods—those men started out with some sense. It was a bunch of clerks and barbers and factory hands from the east that came out here in droves, thought they were getting a good deal. Three things they didn't know sic 'em about: building a shelter and where to find water and fuel to keep from freezing to death." Mr. Malloy waved an arm toward the land. "No logs on the plains, as you can see. Ended up burning their fence posts and furniture. Not many streams, either. If they didn't starve or freeze to death or break down from their labor, they died from the prairie fever."

"What's that?" I asked.

"Typhoid. From drinking bad water. Some folks got so desperate, they resorted to collecting what little water they could find in shallow buffalo wallows."

"Well, my brother started out right," said Dad. "He built his soddy and dug a well, first thing."

"That's the only way," said Mr. Malloy. "You got to know this part of Montana. Extremes in the weather. Nature was good to us until 1917. It rained and wheat soared to two dollars a bushel on account of the war. We got twenty-five bushels to the acre. Best wheat in the country. But the wet years end and the dry come. And along with that, hardships no man can predict. A wind'll blow 'til the land parches and cracks. Not much grass left to hold the soil. Plows have seen to that. We might have to submit a bill to North Dakota for all the topsoil that's likely to blow in there from Montana." Mr. Malloy winked with that comment. "We're already seeing buildings banked with tumble weeds. You think there's rain in a summer cloud. Look again. Might be hail. I'd say this area is ripe for disaster. We'll just have to wait and see what 1920 brings."

The dark closed in on us like a shroud and the land looked like a big lonely nothing with the bleached bones of animal carcasses scattered about. The trail was just as Amer had described it in one of his letters: "a long black ribbon, eerie in the dark, but also one of the most beautiful places I have ever seen."

I felt connected to my uncle that night. As soon as the darkness came down, blacker than black, Montana's huge sky exploded with stars and the horns on grazing steers shone a pearly white in the starlight.

Mr. Malloy stopped the car for a while and turned off the headlights, which, for a brief moment, had caught a mule deer and a few smaller night creatures scurrying off and away. There we were, beneath the same brilliant firmament Amer had loved. A deep, wide sky strung with jewels, like fireworks that never fizzle out. We left the stage and took a few paces toward the edge of our trail. Mr. Malloy invited us to follow him several yards away from the car and onto the uneven prairieland. He spread his arms wide and looked up at the sky.

"Nowhere," he said, "except maybe at sea, do you get this kind of elbow room."

He was right. The sky came down all around at the same distance. We stood there like three small pins on a gigantic map.

"Got to respect it, though. Just like the sea, you never take it for granted. My wife and I took a trip to the Big Snowy Mountains near Lewiston: Greathouse Peak. It's beautiful, of course, but those mountains swallowed us up. Can't imagine living in the Rockies. A man from eastern Montana, well, he feels hemmed in. Needs to come back home and smell the sage."

We sniffed at the air and sure enough, you could have rubbed a Thanksgiving turkey with the scent that night.

Our time in Montana, away from city lights, is something that has stayed with me, even into old age. Years ago, when I walked the streets of Masterton in winter, and Callie and I visited Mother every Tuesday evening, I thought of that Montana sky and those zillions of stars, as Cal would call them. It was a part of Amer's vision. His dream. Gave him a lift, a sense of calm during the short time he lived. As I've often said, it's good for the soul to be at one with the out-of-doors. Makes a fellow feel alive, larger than himself. Distances him from the foolish, petty bickering that goes on in the world of people. Yet, I learned from Mr. Malloy that you never take those surroundings for granted.

We arrived in Jordan late that evening, tired and disheveled from our three days of travel. The town was larger and more populated than I thought it would be. Over 2,000 souls. Mr. Malloy explained that Jordan had grown because of the Homestead boom that began around 1910.

Along either side of the main thoroughfare, a dirt street lined with raised boardwalks, white clapboard buildings seemed to glow in the dark. Our headlights illuminated storefronts and boardinghouses. It was late and not many people were out. The only sounds above our motor were faint music from one of the saloons and a couple of young boys calling out to each other. Dust raised by our car hung in the air once Mr. Malloy stopped in front of the jailhouse.

"I'll wait for you at the hotel while you talk to the sheriff," he said, indicating one of the white buildings in the opposite direction.

The boardwalk stopped several yards before the jail, which was located at the far end of town, half a block off Jordan's Main Street. It was a square building, stout as a fort, with weeds growing up against the concrete foundation. Nearby, a monstrous dead tree stood lopsided, like a giant scarecrow without clothes. Reminded me of a hanging tree.

Built of brick and mortar, the jailhouse was patched in large sections with cement. A slab in front seemed to lead up to a door, but there was only a small barred window. Unsure how to get inside, we circled the structure a couple of times and found a second barred window in the back. The flame from an oil lamp flickered inside. Where was the entry?

Sheriff Fleming, who had sent the telegram, saw us nosing around and stepped out of an obscure rear door to invite us in. He was a gruff, no-nonsense fellow with bushy eyebrows and a thick white mustache. Pinned to his brown vest was a large silver badge—a six-pronged star, imprinted with the word "Sheriff."

I wondered how Dad was going to handle things.

Under the light of a hanging lantern, he looked all tuckered out. Hearing him struggle to find the necessary words disappointed me, made me nervous. But the sheriff said he'd been expecting us and motioned for us to sit down in a pair of sturdy chairs near his desk. He expressed his condolences with a few clipped words, then got down to business—as if dealing with Amer's murder was all in a day's work.

"From the evidence," he said, "your brother was shot with a .45 caliber Colt automatic. It was Tom's gun, all right—a US Army model. My deputy found it on Carmichael's land, hidden in a prairie dog hole."

Just then, we heard a loud, gravelly voice from another part of the jailhouse: "Hey! Hey, out there. Self-defense. It was self-defense!"

With a sneer, Sheriff Fleming muttered, "Not likely."

He stood and clomped over to a connecting door and hollered, "Shut up in there, Tom, or you won't get your breakfast in the morning. Now, shut the hell up!"

Dad was staring at the sheriff with wide eyes bloodshot from lack of sleep.

"What's going on?" I whispered. Dad shook his head.

Here we were just steps away from the man who had murdered Amer. There shouldn't even be a trial, I thought. He should be lynched right now. I'll help string him up on that tree outside. But that's not how the system works, unless a mob takes over. Nevertheless, it was an insult to have to be in the same building as this killer. And with a sheriff who grew less sympathetic as the seconds hammered by on the Seth Thomas wall clock.

Returning to his desk, Sheriff Fleming announced that Tom would remain locked up until his trial, which hadn't been slated yet, and that the deputy would attempt to keep a close watch on the other two Carmichaels.

"They've been hanging around town," he drawled, "stirring up trouble, trying to garner support for Tom. They shouldn't bother you none. Leastwise, I hope not. We sure as hell don't need any more Easterners getting themselves shot around here."

I bristled at the sheriff's comments and at his nonchalant attitude. Scooting forward in my chair, I opened my mouth to speak. If Dad wasn't going to assert himself, then I would. But before I could utter a sound, my father placed a hand on my arm.

"We want to see my brother," he said softly. "And we'd like to see his land."

The sheriff reached for an Eversharp and a tattered black record book, opened it to one of many pages filled with names and numbers, and jotted something he found onto a scrap of paper.

"His claim," he said, "is located two miles north of town. Section forty-six aught thirty-three, acreage twenty-five. You'll find those numbers on the stakes. Lot 11 is where the shooting took place."

Dad thanked him. Too kindly, I thought. But then he made up for it as soon as he rose from the chair. In spite of his exhaustion, he stood up straight and said, "My brother was a good man, Mr. Fleming. A hard worker. He came here to farm, not to get killed."

"Yes, well…I'm sorry," said the sheriff, ushering us out the door and pointing in the direction of the boardwalk. "You'll find the undertaking parlor yonder, past the hotel, inside one of those fancier white-frame buildings at the other end of town. Not very convenient," he snorted, "when a prisoner decides to hang himself here in his cell." He chuckled and adjusted his cowboy hat. "At least it saves on the cost of a trial. Anyhow, the undertaker is expecting you first thing in the morning. Name of Hawkins."

I couldn't wait to get out of that jailhouse. And quickly edged away from the door toward the hanging tree. Dad was close behind.

"By the way," called out Sheriff Fleming, "you might want to talk to the McKammans. They were good friends of your brother. The missus was with him when he died. In the meantime, we'll keep an eye on things here in town."

As we headed in the direction of the hotel, Dad checked his pocket watch. "Ten o'clock," he said. "It's been a long day."

"Three long days," I reminded him. Still aggravated

by the chilly exchange with the sheriff, I added, "That guy should have kept an eye on things before Amer was killed."

Dad clenched his jaw. "I know, son. I know."

In the sultry night, we shuffled along through the dirt and onto the boardwalk. The buildings on Main Street were dark, except for the two saloons and a dim light inside the hotel.

What comfort to find our driver sitting on a bench out front, waiting and watching for us. After our meeting with the sheriff, it was especially heartening to see Mr. Malloy's friendly face again. He smiled and clapped a hand on each of our shoulders as we made for the door.

Like many of the buildings in town, the hotel was a white-frame structure, narrow with three stories. It appeared to include no more than a half dozen rooms, since the lobby and dining room took up the first floor. The check-in area was gloomy and smelled moldy, as if accumulated rainwater had seeped in during the wet years and never completely dried.

Behind a chest-high, gummy wooden counter sat the desk clerk, a puny fellow with round glasses and thin yellowish hair. Not a very likeable sort. Seemed like one of those high-strung, self-important busybodies with nothing worthwhile to back up his patter. Apparently adept at reading the hotel register upside-down, he got all excited over our signatures—hands aflutter as he placed the pen in its holder and capped the inkwell. His voice pitched up an octave and his words came out in staccato.

"Tom Carmichael's brothers are in town," he chattered, waving a copy of the *Jordan Gazette* under our noses. "But Sheriff Fleming and his deputy are watchin' 'em real close. They've got Tom in jail. I don't think you need to worry none. All the same, I'd watch my back if I was you. There could be real trouble. I hear talk of a vigilante committee. Yes, sir, real trouble."

His comments sounded rehearsed, as if he'd been gossiping with everyone who came in. He seemed to be the type who itched to see a shootout on Main Street.

"We'll be fine," Dad told him in his usual slow, calm voice. "All we need is a good night's sleep. *And* a warm breakfast in the morning."

The clerk sniffed and tossed his head. "Rooms around back," he said brusquely. "Up two flights. Breakfast at six."

One of several things I was learning about my dad—made clearer by his exchanges with the sheriff and the desk clerk—he knew how to handle all types with as little fuss as possible.

We carried our bags back outside and felt our way in the dark to a rear staircase, the only way we could get to our rooms, up steep plank steps with no backings and no railings, and in through a small door to a narrow third floor hallway. We had to light a match to see the numbers on the doors. Mr. Malloy's room was directly across from ours. Before turning in for the night, we thanked him heartily for all he had done to help us out.

"We couldn't have managed without you," said Dad.

Accepting our thanks, Mr. Malloy said he'd see us at breakfast and would be glad to stick around while we went to the undertaking parlor.

"And I'll drive you out to Amer's place afterward," he said, shaking our hands. "I'd like to see you through."

"We're mighty grateful," said Dad.

And were we ever. Dad and I had each other, but he'd been so quiet during all that time on the train and in the stage, I often felt as if I were making the trip alone. Although his exhanges with the sheriff and the hotelkeeper gave me a little more confidence, having someone like Mr. Malloy stand by us meant everything. He knew what life was like in that part of the country.

9

Sagebrush Before the Wind

OUR HOTEL ROOM, large and sparsely furnished, was the size of a wing in an old dance hall. Not that I'd ever been inside a dance hall before. But I could imagine floozies and dandies taking a break from their strenuous exercise, fanning themselves, standing around, having a smoke.

In our room, the high ceiling and a scuffed wooden floor seemed to slant off level in opposing directions. The dark floral print wallpaper refused to brighten when I lit the oil lamp on a small table next to the bed. Probably because there wasn't much wick left. The rest of the room's décor consisted of a washstand with a white pitcher etched by tiny dark cracks, a matching basin, one dingy gray washcloth, and a faded blue towel. The water in the pitcher was filmy on the surface.

Beneath the high metal-framed bed sat an old white "thunder mug," as Uncle Amer used to call our chamber pots at home. It was a relief to know that we wouldn't have to go back outside and maneuver those tricky steps in the dark.

Stripped down to our underwear, Dad and I took turns scrubbing ourselves with the chilly water poured into the basin. Then we flopped down onto a bed barely wide enough for one hefty man. Fortunately, we were both thin.

It was hard to settle in for the night. Strange noises came from a room down the hall, a sort of bumping sound, like someone moving furniture. Our mattress was lumpy and sagged toward the floor on my side. Within minutes, we jumped up with a shout, yanked the sheets off the bed, and hustled through the door to shake them out over the railing. Bed bugs. Not that it did much good, shaking off those covers. We wondered if Mr. Malloy was experiencing a similar problem.

After remaking the bed, we lay there in the dark, scratching and talking some more about Amer and the Carmichaels. I suggested buying a gun first thing in the morning. Dad chuckled slightly and said he didn't think we'd need one. His laugh had a bitter edge.

All kinds of thoughts worked my brain that night: I wondered about the mortuary and what Amer would look like dead. Where on his body had he been shot? I'd never seen a human corpse before,only animals. And it made me feel panicky if I thought about him like that for too long. Instead, I imagined Tom Carmichael pacing inside his cell at the county jail, yammering away like when we were there. Would the sheriff withhold his breakfast in the morning? Or maybe the murderer was sleeping, with no remorse.

His brothers weren't implicated, but they'd been hanging around town, acting tough, talking big. That is, if we could believe the hotelkeeper. The town seemed as dark and foreboding as a cave when you have no idea what or who might be lurking deep inside. And just as quiet. After the saloons closed their doors for the night, even the quiet began to unsettle me. The town seemed like a powder keg.

I woke Dad, because the more I thought about our situation, the more I figured we ought to have a gun.

Half awake and groggy, he said, "It might make matters worse. Try not to worry. We have no choice but to trust that the sheriff and his deputy are looking out for us."

"Yeah," I muttered for the second time that night. "The way they looked out for Amer."

I could sense Dad fully awake and staring up at the ceiling after the oil lamp fizzled out. "I know, son," he said quietly. "They didn't do right by him."

Then my father said another thing that has stuck with me ever since. He was never one to go on at any great length about matters, but that night he gave me a rare piece of advice that shed light on how he had dealt with the sheriff and the hotelkeeper: "No matter what the situation, Willie," he said, "no matter what confronts you in life, do what you have to do in a dignified way."

Then he turned onto his side, faced the wall, and told me to get some sleep, because we had a rough day ahead of us.

I relaxed as best I could, confident that my father would be able to deal with the undertaker the next morning—whatever that man's demeanor. More important was how he would react to the sight of his brother.

Seems like I'd just dozed off when it was time to get up. Dad and I took turns using the "thunder mug," then scrubbed our faces in the last bit of cold water from the pitcher before dressing for breakfast. Each of us had packed two changes of clothing: socks, good trousers, underwear, and shirts. Mother had pressed everything for us, even our socks and underwear. You could still catch the faint whiff of her hot iron on wind-dried cloth. I was cheered by changing into clean clothes after all that time on the train and in the stage. How little it takes to comfort a fellow in a tough situation. For me, it was knowing that we still had a set of fresh clothing, pressed and folded by Mother, for our return trip home.

In addition, it was refreshing to step outside and

breathe in that early morning air, exhilarating to see Jordan at daybreak with its bustle of people moving along the boardwalks on either side of a hard-packed Main Street. The town didn't seem as threatening in the new light. The front of our hotel seemed more welcoming, painted white with pale green trim and the name Jordan Hotel lettered in black across the top like a billboard.

Daylight provided us with a panorama of this boom town, the Garfield county seat: hotel, general store, lumber mill, post office, rooming houses, and two saloons. At the far end, beyond the jailhouse, a blacksmith shop stood next door to a livery stable. I never took much notice of those buildings the night before. Several children with neatly combed hair were skipping along the street toward a sod schoolhouse on the outskirts of town called Vail Creek School. Girls in middy dresses, and boys wearing short pants and jackets, carried lunch pails and strapped books.

What is it about the light of day? No matter where you are in the world, when things are at their bleakest, good old Sol, a row of bright buildings, lively children, and a greeting or two from strangers work wonders. Neutralizers that help chase away the dread. Although we had yet to meet with the mortician and view Amer's body, my concern for our own safety and the near-desperate uncertainty I'd felt in the middle of the night inside that dark hotel room waned—

edged out by a clear sky and the promise of sunshine. And the delicious smells of breakfast cooking.

Mr. Malloy was already inside the dining room, visiting with another hotel guest and several ranchers whose horses we'd noticed as we came down the rear steps and around to the front door. A few more cowboys rode up, dismounted, and tied off their reins at the hitching rails where a long row of patient chestnut, black, paint, and buckskin horses stood shoulder-to-shoulder, a hint of fresh trail dust coating their hindquarters. Boots clomped on the boardwalk and spurs jingled as a dozen men, farmers and ranchers, joined us in the dining room that morning. Word had gotten out about Amer's kin from Minnesota.

With somber nods, they shook our hands and removed their hats, as if at a funeral visitation. Then we sat down together at a large oblong table and waited for our food.

Breakfast was served family style: platters heaped with thick slices of roast pork and beef, fried eggs, sunny side up, bowls of steaming potatoes, gravy and pork drippings, buttered biscuits, pails of hot coffee. The food was good, but I didn't have much appetite. It didn't seem right to sit at a table among all those men without Amer. No place setting for Amer. That he should be lying inside the mortuary just a little way down the street from us, four days dead, was... well, I couldn't find a word for the awful feeling it gave me.

A glance around the table made it obvious which of

the men likely had a wife or sister at home. Those were the scrubbed ones with trimmed hair, clean clothes, and a fresh bandanna around the neck. The rest all seemed the same— lean, grim, sunburnt, dull-eyed, worn out. A couple of them had the look of men who'd lost too many spring crops to hail. I've seen plenty of those over the years—farmers forced to stand by helpless while their young corn plants got shredded and beaten to the ground. All those weeks of labor. Never saw them give up, though. They'd return to their fields next day, ready to replant.

Against the quiet, you could hear several horses nickering at their hitching posts. The soft clatter of breakfast dishes and the occasional shuffling of boots beneath the table were the only sounds inside.

These men had ridden in that morning out of curiosity, but they were also there to pay their respects and to tell us what they knew about Amer and the Carmichaels. You could sense their tacit sympathy. When they finally spoke, it was with an abruptness similar to Mr. Malloy's.

Halfway through our meal, one of the men started up about how a Homestead fight affected everyone, made them all jittery. Then, one after another, each man had his say:

"The Carmichaels don't like fences. And they don't like cattle."

"You interfere with the way they see fit to running things, they'll come after you."

"Mean cusses, especially Tom. Just as soon shoot you as look at you."

"They have a reputation around here for letting their sheep graze everybody out."

"That's for sure. Those boys drift with their stock and when one section is used up, they move on to the next. Hell, they don't care whose land it is."

"About your brother, Mr. Lindstrom," said one with thin, cigarette-scarred lips, "it was more than a Homestead fight. It got personal."

"Personal?" said another, shaking his head. "I don't know...."

"Hell, yes. There was no doubt where the stakes were on Amer's claim. I'll say it again—it got personal."

"I think that's true," said a rancher with worried eyes and deep creases at the corners. "He tried to stand up to Tom, but he... you see, out here, some folks pick on them that's soft."

"He wasn't one to take hard liquor, your brother. Other'n that, he was an all right sort of fella."

A few of the men chuckled over that comment.

"All I can say is we've had enough of them Carmichael boys. I'd sure as hell like to get on that jury. Just as soon see him hang."

As quickly as those men started talking, they fell quiet—everything of importance having been said—and ate the rest of their meal in silence, with old hands. The only sound left was the scraping of flatware against crockery. Those last spoken words lingered in my mind: "Just as soon see him hang."

For a second, I pictured a faceless man with a noose around his neck, dangling from "the hanging tree" near the jailhouse.

Dad and I had learned more from those locals and settlers at breakfast than from Sheriff Fleming the night before. Had Carmichael really accused Amer of claiming a portion of land that he, Carmichael, said was rightfully his? Or was there more to it? Why hadn't the sheriff told us any of this? Moreover, why hadn't my dad asked questions?

What troubled me was the notion of Amer being called soft. He was a gentleman, true, but he could stand up for himself when he had to. I never took him for a pushover. He was a crack shot at trap. And he pitched a hell of a game for the Hadley Buttermakers. What was the real reason for his murder? And why hadn't the law stepped in, especially after that awful beating?

When it came time for our appointment with the undertaker, Dad stood and thanked everyone for joining us and for their kind words about Amer. Before leaving the dining room, I took one last look at the gaunt, sinewy builds of those ranchers and settlers. Their finger-combed hair and pale brows and work-worn hands. They glanced up at us as we turned to go.

Without expecting an answer, one said, "Will we ever see his like again?" Then they sent us on our way with quick nods and went back to the task at hand—mopping up egg yolk with chunks of biscuit.

Outside the hotel, we had to stop on the boardwalk and shield our faces from a sudden gust that whipped up small brush and clouds of dust. Then a whirl of wind put on quite a show, spinning and dancing the length of Main Street, chasing down brittle brown tumbleweeds and bowling them from one end of town to the other.

"Sagebrush before the wind," said Dad, peeking around the edge of his coat collar.

Those words carried a double significance that day. Long ago, he used them to describe his four brothers and himself, abandoned by their father, orphaned by the deaths of their mother and sister. "We all went our separate ways," he used to say, "like sagebrush before the wind.

10

It's Only The Shell, Willie

OUR PATH TO THE UNDERTAKER'S PARLOR was not a smooth one. Halfway along the boardwalk, we came upon two rough-looking men slouched on a bench in front of the General Store. I knew right away who they were.

Those thugs didn't even have to say a word. Their surly, rotten attitudes showed through by the way they sat. Hooligans. Up to no good. Dad and I slowed our pace. Just like in an old western shoot-'em-up, we had our rotters ready to stir up trouble. And a sheriff, a little ways down the street, leaning against a hitching post, arms folded across his chest, trying to look nonchalant. As soon as Sheriff Fleming saw that we were aware of his presence, he reached up and pushed the brim of his cowboy hat back with his thumb.

The Carmichael brothers sneered and glared at us with expressions as wicked as a man can conjure this side of Hell. Teeth like yellowed Chiclets. Leathery faces the color of beef jerky. Filthy cowboy hats. I checked their sides for guns, but saw no holsters. Who knew? They might have concealed Derringers or Bowie knives inside their boots. One of them stretched his arms wide, yawned, and stuck his long legs straight out, forcing us to sidestep. I stopped and looked the guy full in the face. Mean? I have never in my entire life seen eyes like his. Onyx hard, like a snake's. I didn't know which brother I was staring down, Seth or Jim, but I felt like spitting on his dusty boots. He stood up and slowly came toward me, clenching his fists and pinning me with the look of a baited bull.

"Somethin' ailing you, kid?" he said, spitting tobacco juice on the boardwalk near my feet.

Halfway hypnotized, I stared back, speechless, blind to the chance I was taking. But as soon as the sheriff started down the street in our direction, that bully stopped, tensed up, and shifted his attention away from me.

Dad took hold of my arm and steered me along the boardwalk, away from those men.

"Stay calm, Willie," he whispered. "Don't show any fear."

But I was more angry than afraid—and a bit cocky.

Natural for a sixteen-year-old kid. I turned and nailed that guy with the fiercest look I could muster, focusing on his beak of a nose instead of those snake eyes. Just then, the sheriff came running with a shout, "Hold it right there, Jim!"

Seconds later, a shot rang out! Hunkering down, with hearts racing, Dad and I scurried behind the post office. Dogs barked. A woman screamed and darted past us. After a minute of dead silence, we peeked around the corner.

Jim Carmichael, still seated on the bench, now with his hands raised, had evidently reached into his boot. His pant leg was still pulled up. I didn't see any weapons, but the sheriff handcuffed both men and hustled them off to jail. Sheriff Fleming had called out his warning, then fired his revolver, presumably in the air. My heart pounded for a long time after that.

*   *   *

"Oh, William!" cries Hannah, edging forward on her bench. "That was an awful chance you took! Why, just imagine, you and Vic might have been shot on your way to the mortuary. Oh, dear Lord...."

Nellie fans her face with an old church bulletin she's dug out of her purse. "I can't even begin to think of something like that happening here in Rockford," she says, her upper lip beading with sweat.

"Or back home in Minnesota," says Cal. "Can you picture a shootout on Masterton's Main Street, Dad?"

I thought of the man who had killed his wife and mother-in-law in front of the Catholic Church a half block from our house, many years ago. Difference was—the women were unarmed and dressed in their Sunday best.

"Guess a murder can happen anywhere. In hindsight, ladies, it's probably a good thing we didn't have a gun back in Jordan or I might not have lived to tell this tale."

Hannah reaches over to give Cal a hug. "Goodness gracious, to think we might never have known your dear, sweet daughter."

Nellie stands and stretches. Places her hands against the small of her back.

"I'm getting awfully stiff, Will. I think we should go back to the house, finish up over refreshments."

"Oh, hush, Nellie," says Hannah. "You heard what the man said. He'll not be telling Uncle Amer's story over teacups and lace doilies. Wouldn't be fitting. Now sit down. I want to hear the rest."

"Well, I declare!" spouts Nellie.

I grin and wink at Hannah who smiles back.

"Declare all you want, Nell. Move around a bit if you like, but we're not leaving this cemetery until I get to the end of my story. It's the least we can do for him."

The rest of us stand and stretch. After a few jumping

jacks, Cal saunters over to the big cottonwood tree. I half expect her to start climbing its branches. If ever there's a tree to scale, she'll give it a go, even at her age.

My cousins straighten out their handkerchiefs on the bench's wooden slats and lower themselves once again, as if aiming for a target. Cal plops down on the grass with her back against the tree trunk. Pieces of last summer's cottonwood fluff float through the air. A robin sings. The sun is heading far into the west.

I sit down again with a freshly lit pipe. One more bowl of sweet tobacco should be sufficient to see us through to the end.

"Now where was I?"

"On your way to the undertaking parlor," says Cal, glancing up at my cousins. "Though I don't think any of us really wants to go there."

"Yah, yah," says Hannah. "It seems we've been avoiding the inevitable."

I draw on the stem of my pipe while sifting through the last of Amer's letters stacked on the bench next to me. "Yes, well, it wasn't easy."

*   *   *

After that unnerving business with the Carmichaels and the gunshot on Main Street, my heart was still in my throat as we approached the stoop of yet another white frame building. This one reflected greater investment and outward upkeep than the others—fresh paint, a picket fence, flowers around the foundation. A lucrative undertaking, that business.

I jumped a foot when I heard, then saw who was behind the door. Before Dad could knock, the hinges creaked and a creepy voice said, "I've been watching for you. Come in, please. For a moment, I thought I'd have more customers coming my way."

We didn't laugh and neither did he. Soon found out he wasn't the joking kind.

It was as dim inside that entry as a darkened nickelodeon, where your eyes are slow to adjust and you can hear the racing notes of a violin or a piano playing along with Buster Keaton's antics. But here, there were no gaudy posters or the sounds of a piano or a violin. And no comedy. Instead, the undertaker materialized from behind the door. His looks matched his voice.

Mr. Hawkins was tall and thin, angular, dressed in black—a suit too tight, even for a skinny man. He had a long, narrow face and a high forehead. He wasn't exactly bald, but it was a long stretch before you saw the hairline. He fixed us with strange, pool-like eyes, as if he had gazed too long at his work. His smile, when it relaxed, twisted into an odd grimace. Tilting his head, he bowed slightly, then walked over to a small table with a lamp on it. He seemed a touch too practiced, as if he were following his undertaker's manual to a *T*. Here was a keeper of the dead and he gave me the willies.

Mr. Hawkins struck a match and lit the wick of a hurricane lamp. After adjusting the flame, slowly replacing its chimney, then readjusting the flame, he took up the lamp and motioned for us to follow him as he *oiled* his way from the darkened parlor, along a narrow corridor, through a tiny door (we had to duck to avoid hitting our heads on a rafter), and down rough-hewn steps. Despite the warm, dry weather, the basement was dank. Our sunshiny day was forgotten once we'd gone down into that musty cellar.

The lamp threw eerie shadows against clay walls and over a hard-packed dirt floor. Except for the peculiar odors, the place reminded me of our root cellar back home. Instead of giving off the smells of stored carrots and squash and apples, this damp room smelled of saltpeter, like an ancient cemetery on a rainy night when the faint odor of decaying corpses rises up through the ground.

At first, I was appalled to find my uncle in a dirt basement. But then, I thought, why not? Amer had been a farmer all his life. Nearly everything of importance to him was of the earth—his soddy, those dusty trails, the land he worked, even the burial plot waiting for him in Rockford.

It all made sense. Why not an earthen mortuary? As Amer would likely have said, "It is clean dirt."

My eyes soon adjusted to the gloom and to the rows of cosmetics and pastes lined up on a narrow table against one wall. Against another wall stood a tall desk with a three-by-three-foot Coroner's Book. Strange paraphernalia hung from large hooks pounded into the clay—most likely embalming tubes and such. The smell of formaldehyde made me nauseous and a little woozy. I expected Dad would feel the same, but he stood tall with an expression that hadn't changed since breakfast. Or, for that matter, since we'd received the terrible news three days ago. I'd felt lonely, irritated even, that my father had so little to say during our train trip and the journey from Forsyth to Jordan with Mr. Malloy at the wheel. But by the time we left the hotel that morning, I remembered what he had told me the night before. And I realized he was trying to stay calm and steady for my sake. I looked to him and held onto his strength inside that awful cellar.

Mr. Hawkins carried his oil lamp toward the center of the room and hung it from a hook in the beamed ceiling, directly above a jerry-rigged table with a cloth draped over it. Beneath the white cloth lay my uncle's lifeless form.

By age sixteen, I'd shot plenty of game and held dead and dying animals. But I'd never seen a dead person. I was curious. At the same time I didn't want to see him like that.

Maybe there was some mistake and this wasn't Uncle Amer. Wouldn't it be wonderful, I thought, if this were a mix-up and he had simply left to go fishing at Fort Peck Lake without telling anyone? Just as I'd imagined on the train, this could be a case of mistaken identity. Although unusual and far-fetched, things like that do happen. Don't they?

Mr. Hawkins pinched the top corners of the sheet between thumbs and index fingers. With a slow flourish, as if unveiling a work of art, he peeled back the cover.

My legs began to tremble and my heart beat so hard I could hear my own pulse throbbing in my head. Blood surged like a whitewater river through my arteries.

Naked, except for a cloth draped across his privates, Uncle Amer's straight-limbed body lay there, thin—skeletal thin—making him appear taller than he actually was. His torso was the color of flax, which made his face, lower neck, forearms and hands look all the more sunburnt, like shades of copper. His hair was swept back, revealing a white forehead. I was shocked by the peaceful look on his face; as if he hadn't known any violence. He seemed vulnerable and alone, lonely even, yet wanting privacy. I felt as though we had intruded.

Mr. Hawkins urged us to step closer. Both Dad and I bristled at the sight of the bullet holes.

The undertaker matter-of-factly pointed out and explained each one: "Your brother was shot twice with a .45

caliber," he said. "He took the first in the abdomen. The fatal bullet grazed his right arm and went in three inches below the nipple on the left side, over the seventh rib, then ranged downward, coming out toward the back of the eleventh rib. It penetrated the lung and passed just below the heart."

The wounds were clean, but the holes were large. The skin around them had turned black. Mr. Hawkins said that as he was undressing Amer, one of the flattened bullets tumbled from his clothes. He took it over to Sheriff Fleming.

"The bullets hadn't hit any vital organs, except for the lung," said the mortician. "That's why your brother didn't die right away. He would have experienced much pain on breathing. It's possible he could have been saved, if he'd received immediate help. If we'd had the means. I'm sorry to say he simply bled out."

"Could have been saved, if…" is not something you like to hear. What good did that comment do us? Dad slowly shook his head and moved in closer.

As long as I live, I'll never forget what happened next. Just as Mr. Hawkins began telling us he'd ready the rough box and corpse for the long journey back to Rockford, Dad leaned over the slab and gathered Amer in his arms. Making little choking sounds, he held his brother tight against his chest for a long time before he could bear to ease him back onto the table. Tenderly, he touched the skin around each of the bullet holes, then drew the sheet up around Amer's shoulders and neck as if he were tucking him in for the night. He lightly brushed his rough brown fingers across Amer's paper-white forehead.

When Dad finally turned to look at me, his eyes glistened, but his expression had changed. For the first time in three days, he took on that clenched look I saw on the faces of the ranchers back at the hotel. Then his eyes brimmed, and turned from pale blue to nearly white.

I fought the urge to cry. And when my legs began to buckle, Dad reached an arm around my waist. He steadied me and bolstered me up until I could hold my ground. I can feel it to this day—my father's strength. It coursed through me like the current from a trickle charger.

"This is just the shell of him, Willie," he whispered. "Always remember that. It's only the shell."

I have never forgotten what my father taught me that day: When someone dies, the casing is all that's left. What is essential rises up out of that shell to become a part of the whole.

"As long as we remember," he said, trying to keep his lips from quivering, "the dead are never dead."

I had more growing up to do before those words could really take hold.

As we turned to go back up the narrow steps, I glanced one last time at Uncle Amer lying there on that slab. In spite of what Dad had just told me, I felt as though we were abandoning him. I did not want to turn my back on my uncle. And to think that Mother and Ray would never have the chance to say their goodbyes, not even at the funeral in Rockford.

Although it hurt my eyes, I was glad to see the light of day when we climbed up out of that cellar. Mr. Hawkins said little else, just that he'd have a pine box set to go whenever we were ready to leave Jordan. He showed us out the same way we'd come in.

I began to breathe easier when I saw Mr. Malloy waiting for us in front of the hotel. This time, he was standing with several townspeople who had gathered around to admire his stage and wanted to talk about what had happened on Main Street. While Mr. Malloy showed them the engine and explained how to start it, Dad and I collected our things from inside the hotel and paid for the night's lodging. Dad paid for Mr. Malloy's room, as well. The desk clerk said nothing about the Carmichaels' arrest or the sheriff's warning shot or how it must have affected us. He simply thanked my father in the same clipped manner as the night before.

The drive to Amer's land took about half an hour through dust and dryland vegetation: sagebrush, buckwheat, and western wheatgrass. Mr. Malloy also pointed out a yellow-flowered plant called curlycup gumweed, which the Indians used for medicinal purposes.

"The bees like it, too," he said. "Makes good honey."

There were shrubs called greasewood, found in alkaline soil, which reminded me of the old geezer off the trail between Forsyth and Jordan—the guy with the gun and the whiskey bottle.

I asked how any crops could grow without irrigation during such a dry spell.

"They don't," said Mr. Malloy. "After the rains stopped and the drought began, nothing could thrive. Just look at the farmers' faces. That'll tell you. Conditions have become severe. And they'll likely grow worse."

Amer's 'dobe and timbered corral rose up in the distance like a tiny fort. As we drew nearer, it became obvious that the place was abandoned. With the horses gone, there was no sign of life, not even a bird. And no Radge to herd any of 'em. Where was that frisky dog Amer had written about?

You could smell the hot sun cooking the earth and dried cornstalks. At several spots next to his fields, Amer had piled mounds of stones he'd cleared from his land before he could get in to work the soil and plant his crops. Heaps of boulders like you'd find at ancient burial sites.

I hesitated before entering the sod house. Here was everything of importance to my uncle, his past and his hopes for the future, the door to his world, inside and out. It didn't feel right to walk in without Amer there to greet us, to show us around, eager and proud of all the hard work he and his horses had done together. I turned to look at the acres of corn they'd planted. But the soil and the crops were parched, dwarfed, barely recognizable. So unlike our fields of tall, green rows at home.

"Just sit back now boys and watch 'em grow," Amer used to say. Wasn't going to happen here.

Still, I could see what he loved about this place. Day and night that enormous sky and broad horizon, as wide as it was deep, soaring over the land version of an ocean. The packed glitter of stars. The sun rising and setting on the acreage he worked. How small is a man under all of that? Convinced of its possibilities, Amer had been willing to drive himself until he broke. For starters, here was his planting, albeit wilted and thirsting for rain. And here was the solid earthen home he had built for himself with the aid of a turf cutter and a wheelbarrow. And generous help from John and Mary McKamman.

"Like they do in Ireland," explained Mr. Malloy. "You have to clear the upper layers of stems and tough roots before you can cut your bricks." He demonstrated the motions with an imaginary turf spade. "Make your cut on two sides, like this. Then with a single twist you've got a brick."

He held out his hands to show the dimensions of a size-able slab of sod, then dusted his palms as if he'd just stacked a row of bricks. "The top layers we use for fuel."

On a rickety crate near the entry sat a clay pot filled with dried soil tamped around withered brown stems, brittle leaves and faded flowers, except for one red blossom that spoke geranium.

I stepped inside the 'dobe, immediately struck by how comfortable Amer had made it. Those sod bricks were evenly stacked, the cracks filled with soaked newspaper, rags, and mud. The hard-packed floor didn't even resemble dirt. Sprinkled with water and swept often, it had become free of dust and hard as cement. Amer had plastered the walls with a mixture of clay and ashes for a whitewash effect and reinforced the ceiling with timbers and tarpaper in order to support the sod roof. A few stringy roots dangled from above the rafters, but because of the drought, no rainwater had as yet seeped through the inevitable cracks and holes. No puddles. No streaks of mud. It was a fine shelter, dry, well-chinked, homey, ready for winter.

Because he lived alone, Amer had no reason to partition his space with blankets for privacy. It remained one large room, neat and clean. His narrow bed was made up with a brightly colored quilt, likely stitched together by Mary McKamman. A single wooden chair and a small table, covered with a clean square of blue-flowered oilcloth, stood against one wall. The oilcloth reminded me of our long table back home—once strewn with maps and railroad brochures in a kitchen alive with chatter and excitement over Amer's plans.

Beneath the table lay a small trap door with an iron ring.

I shoved the table aside, raised the door, and looked down into a dark hole. The air was cool inside a recess big enough for a large crock of milk, which Dad and I lifted up onto the table along with several pounds of butter, a few potatoes, and jars of butchered meat in brine.

"We'll see that the McKammans get all this food," he said.

I placed the cover back over the now empty hole, then explored the rest of the room.

There, on a homemade shelf, were his books with faded blue and green and gray spines aligned as perfectly as a row of corn: Shakespeare, Cervantes, Longfellow, Cooper, Willa Cather, Jonathan Swift, Dickens. I imagined Uncle Amer reading and re-reading these volumes, especially in winter, when there would be little else to do except look after the animals and wait for spring to break through. Warm and cozy. I wondered, though, at the fifty-gallon drum filled with kerosene so old it was the color of Mars.

*   *   *

"Oh, no," says Nellie, abruptly. "He used kerosene inside that soddy?"

Hannah shakes her head. "Bad stuff. Our uncle Benoni had one of those drums inside his little bachelor shack in Davis Junction. That's how he kept warm in winter."

"Burning kerosene in closed quarters?" asks Cal. "Isn't that really dangerous?"

"I should say so!" says Hannah. "It was cheap heat and not uncommon years ago. But over time the fumes made people sick. Uncle Benoni, for example. He was always feeling poorly."

"He smelled funny, too," says Nell. "His clothes and skin. I'm sure it was the kerosene seeping from his pores. He was so thin and pale. We couldn't help but feel sorry for the poor man."

"Didn't you encourage him to stop using it?" asks Cal. "It would have been safer to burn wood."

"Oh, no. He was an old bachelor. We would never have thought to tell him how to live his life."

Cal and I exchange glances. What is it about Nell's remark that doesn't fly with us?

11

His Master's Face

WITH MR. MALLOY'S HELP, Dad and I faced the grim task of packing up Uncle Amer's belongings: the family pictures, a couple dozen books, his shaving mug and brush—the same things he had packed when he left our farm in Hadley. As for the implements and tools purchased in Forsyth and Jordan, those would go to the McKammans.

We packed his phonograph and the dark red album storage book embossed with Victor Records and its trademark painting of Nipper, his ear cocked before the horn, listening intently to a recording of his dead master's voice. Inside the album, well-worn sleeves contained Amer's prized celluloids, including Enrico Caruso singing *Tosca* and Florence Easton's character, Lauretta, singing *"O Mio Babbino Caro."*

"Just because that aria belongs to a woman," Amer once said, "I see no reason a man can't sing it, too, if he feels like it. Especially out in his fields with no one there to correct him."

The violin that had accompanied his singing was the last to leave the soddy, its smooth, scuffed wood coated with a thin layer of dust. And its frets a little grimy with seasons of in-grained dirt. Dad carefully wrapped it in Amer's blue chambray work shirt. Just as he was nesting it on top of the luggage at the rear of the stage, the McKammans arrived, having walked the distance from their homestead.

John's sunburned, freckled face shone with good health. His pale red hair held a neat part on the right side. He wore fresh work clothes. Except for one thing, John resembled the ranchers and farmers who had ridden into town for breakfast that morning. The noticeable difference—merry eyes, twinkling and cheery.

And so were the eyes of Mary McKamman. She stood tall and sturdy with grayish brown hair pulled back tightly in a bun. Her broad smile revealed deep dimples. She immediately reached out to give me a strong, motherly hug, then kept an arm around my shoulders for an extra moment. I could see why Uncle Amer liked her. She and John were every bit as good-hearted as he had described them in his letters—the kind of people you want to be around because they give you the feeling that anything is possible, that any hardship can be overcome. Hope and an indomitable spirit. That's what the McKammans were made of. And they set out to lift ours.

"It's powerful sorry we are," said John, shaking Dad's hand and then my own, as well as Mr. Malloy's.

"We're missing him every day," said Mary. "Early of a morning, I look for Amer out workin' a section with those four horses and Radge trotting alongside. Stayed close by, he did."

I asked where Radge was. John said they had taken him in, along with the horses, but had to tether him to a stake because he kept running back to look for Amer.

"Can't you hear him, then?" he asked, cupping an ear.

I listened and caught the sound of a mid-sized dog barking a short distance away.

"A smart one, he is. About this high." John lowered his hand towards the ground. "A fine Border Collie, black and white."

"Suren, that Radge is a fine dog," said Mrs. McKamman. "But he misses his master. Runs off in search of him whenever he gets the chance. Well, then, when you've finished here, John and I would have you come by our place for coffee and eats."

With the last of Amer's possessions piled on the rear seat of the stage, I closed the soddy door, wondering what would become of this little house. Would it fall to ruin or would another honyocker eventually move in—another farmer as eager as Amer to carve out a place for himself in Eastern Montana? Whoever entered wouldn't find it completely empty. There would be that old kerosene stove the color of Mars. And the makeshift bookshelf.

During one last look around, I noticed a gleam coming from one corner of the shelf, gold lettering on the spine of a single volume propped in the shadows. Its dark brownish green binding blended with the wood. The cover was beautiful. Embossed vines and leaves and golden roots trailed from the title, **Leaves of Grass**. I opened it to the 1855 copyright page and then read a little of the first poem, "Song of Myself." The third line stood out: "For every atom belonging to me as good belongs to you."

I might have taken those poems, but everything else had been packed and tied down inside the stage. Something about that book. It just seemed right to let it be. So I left it for whoever might occupy Amer's shelter in years to come.

Mr. Malloy started up his Cadillac. Dad helped John and Mary get into the middle seat. Then he and I took our usual places next to our driver. But Mr. Malloy didn't leave right away. He sat there for a moment with his hands on the wheel, letting the car idle as he gazed at the soddy. Before we could ask if there was a problem or if we'd forgotten something, he got out of the car and walked over to the well, took down the large pewter ladle hanging from a hook, and dipped water from the little bit left on the bottom of the horse trough. Was he going to drink that? No. He returned to the soddy and poured the water onto the dying geranium.

Dad brought his hand to his mouth. No one spoke.

Mr. Malloy returned the ladle to its hook, got back in the car, and drove the half mile to the McKammans' soddy. The rest of us held on our laps many of the things that would soon belong to them: kitchen supplies, food, clothing, small implements.

The shotgun we would take home with us, back to Hadley. Never did find the revolver.

Eight horses, including Amer's, stood corralled next to the road. They were nicely filled out, muscular, with coats shining in the sun. My uncle wrote about how he loved the smell of horses in the rain. And during a good brushing after long hours in the fields. He'd treated them well and it showed. In return, he said, they'd given him their best. Amer's four stood still looking at us with knowing eyes. If they could talk, what would they tell us?

Radge, alert to our arrival, leapt up and down, barking in excitement, shaking the dust from his coat. I laughed at the smiling snout Amer had so accurately described in his letters, that happy grin as the dog cut and run and chased those evening birds across the fields. As soon as I hopped out of the stage, he stopped jumping and strained at his tether, desperate for attention. He hunkered low and wagged his tail, inviting me to play. Right then and there, I wanted to take that pup home with us. I could tell my brother the dog was meant for him. Then maybe he wouldn't feel so bad about having to stay back on the farm.

I played with Radge for a few minutes, and then sat down on the ground while he rested his muzzle on my knee. With one stroke of his thick coat, it became obvious that he was still sore where his ribs had been broken by Tom Carmichael's boot. He looked up at me with such eyes and whimpered when I tethered him again.

I wouldn't have left the dog, only I didn't want to miss out on what the McKammans had to say about Amer's last hours. Because the bullets hadn't hit any vital organs, other than one lung, he lived long enough to tell his side of the story. If only he could have made it to a hospital. But there wasn't any close by. So, as Mr. Hawkins said, he just bled out. Bled out while describing his own murder.

Around seven o'clock on the morning Amer was shot, he and John and Tom Carmichael went out to their respective fields. John McKamman planting corn. Amer with four horses hitched to a disk drill, working his oblong field near a division marker. Instead of settling into his own labor, Carmichael paced up and down the fence line on the adjacent land, acting testy, lashing out at his team. "Screaming at the air like one possessed," is how John described him.

Amer ignored the whole scene and kept at his work. Around noon, he tried to get through the common gate, but couldn't without great difficulty. Carmichael had deliberately wired it shut with doubled hogwire, staples, and a web halter strap to delay Amer's getting out when he broke for dinner. When Tom rode up with his .45 drawn and cocked, Amer ran back to his team for the rifle. But before he could get at the saddle holster, Tom fired that first shot. It grazed Amer's arm and lodged in his stomach. He doubled over and took cover behind the horses, but they got excited and milled out of control. Tom squeezed off a second bullet, the one that entered Amer's chest, then turned sharply and galloped away without making sure he had shot him dead. His rifle still askew in the saddle holster, Amer lay bleeding there on the ground, while his horses nuzzled him.

"Suren, if only he'd had his revolver," said John. "Why he left it behind, we'll always wonder. It was more than once those Carmichaels taunted and threatened him fierce. Shoved him off the footpath. Then that awful beating."

Dad didn't say anything about not finding the gun. Someone must have gone into the soddy and taken it.

"That Carmichael," said Mary. "The look of the man I never liked." She curled the edge of her apron as if rolling a bandage. "Oh, the face on him. The eyes. Hungry for the land and no heart. The way he drives his sheep, whippin' 'em as if they was mules. Beyond the pale, it is."

"I know Amer was a crack shot," said John. "A fine trap shooter back in Minnesota. Suren, he could have picked Carmichael off at long range."

"Och, aye, 'tis a shame." Mary slowly shook her head. "But he didn't have it in him."

"True it is." John poured a little of his coffee from cup to saucer, then sipped the cooled liquid, holding the saucer between his thumb and two fingers.

"Radge barked like fury," he said, setting the saucer back on the square wooden table. "Then the gunshots. We ran down the road and saw Amer stooped over, hugging his chest. He staggered and dropped, then picked himself up and made a few more paces before falling down again. By the time we reached him, he was crawling along the fence line with Radge tight by his side. He took off his work gloves, full of dust and blood they were, and passed them to Mary."

"Calm-like, he asked us to take him to town—to the doctor."

With pinched lips, John gazed at his wife for a moment before continuing.

"Another neighbor came a-running. Mr. Armstrong. Fought in the Great War, he had. Tended plenty of the injured. Mr. Armstrong took one look at Amer's wounds and told him he wouldn't live long enough to make it to Jordan. Sometimes it hurts to be honest. But honest is how he had to be.

"Mary keeps a store of medicines and bandages, so we loaded your one into Armstrong's Chevrolet and drove the half mile back here to our soddy with Radge running alongside. Armstrong was right. Amer couldn't have stood the longer ride into town. His only chance would be to get the doctor back to our place in time to remove the bullets and patch him up before too much blood flowed out. We placed him on the bed. He wasn't very heavy. Armstrong and I drove apace into town for the sheriff and the doctor. We went together, our revolvers at the ready, in case Carmichael and his brothers lurked nearby. Mary stayed by Amer."

"And Radge, too," she said. "Och, the terrible pain. He tried to bear up, your one. Aye, he fixed his hands on his chest, just so. But suren, it got the better of him."

To this day, I can hear Mary's sweet voice, her Irish brogue. And I can see her otherwise cheerful eyes tear up as she told us about Amer's last moments.

"I did what I could to comfort him," she said softly. "Gentle he was, our dear, dear friend. Never wishin' to sow harm upon a soul. 'Suren, Mr. Lindstrom,' I says, 'you'll be pullin' through this. You've got work aplenty to do on your place.'

"He spoke witness." Mary McKamman reached for her worn, black leather Bible and opened it to the page where she had recorded his testimony. "It's all here, it is. He even put down his name."

I could have wept when she read us his words: "I, Amer Lindstrom, expecting to die, do make this statement, true, so help me God."

"After the signing," said Mary, "Amer whispered something I'll remember all my days, I will. He said, 'I guess Tom Carmichael didn't care for my music.'"

Where had I heard that before?

"Would Amer had his revolver," said John, "he might have stood a chance. But you know, Mr. Lindstrom, my Mary is right. Your brother just didn't have it in him to fight."

"He struggled and poured sweat would he be working a field at midday," said Mary. "Every breath he took made him double up. Cry out in pain. Radge cried, too, and turned in tight circles. I did my best to soothe Amer. Washed the dirt and dust from his face and hands. Stroked his arms—those he still held tight to his chest. He bled through all the bandages, so I used feed sack towels to pack the wounds and staunch the bleeding.

"After a time, he settled down and stared up into my face like he was searching for something. His eyes—soft, they were. And wide open. Such beautiful clear blue eyes."

Mary shook her head slowly. "I'll never forget our dear Swede, Amer Lindstrom. Lovely, he was. I gave him back my tenderest smile. You see, I thought he might be remembering his mother; and, would I do that, why, it would help ease him out and into the next. He used to talk about his mother, you know—Ernestine. Said she died young. Left a good number of children, she did."

Mary McKamman stopped talking in order to collect herself. John reached over to pat her hand. After dabbing at her eyes with a corner of her apron, she continued.

"Radge stood by the whole time, whining softly at the end. Nudging him with his nose. Amer tried so hard to stay, but it was no good. He looked like a boy, really. A tired boy just in from the fields and ready for a good rest. He gazed down at his dog for a time and drifted off to sleep. After a bit, he stopped breathing."

As Mary whispered those last words to the rest of us gathered around her table, the sun edged toward the horizon. Dust motes traveled slowly along a shaft of light burning in through a rippled windowpane.

She explained how she had gently closed my uncle's eyes with her fingertips, and placed coins on his eyelids. When she drew the blanket up over Amer's face, Radge whined and pawed at the cover. Mary quickly lowered the blanket and comforted the dog until he settled down.

"You understand," she said, "that dog wasn't ready for his master's face to be hidden from sight."

The two of them kept vigil. Mary in her straight-back chair, Radge standing next to the low bed with his muzzle resting on Amer's arm.

"We waited like that," she said, "until John and Mr.

Armstrong returned with the sheriff and the doctor."

For a long moment, the five of us sat silent, listening to Amer's dog barking outside. A sudden wind whistled through the cracks between the window frames and sod walls. The lowering sun caught a few dust motes still circling in the light.

John spoke in low tones. "He's caught rotten now, is Tom."

Dad nodded once and lifted his cup for a final swallow of strong coffee. He stood and thanked the McKammans for their kindness, said he'd never forget all they had done for his brother, and reminded them to keep the animals, the timbers from their corral, and Amer's farm equipment and tools.

"Mind yourselves now," said John. "Safe journey."

Taking leave of the McKammans was as difficult as any goodbye I've ever experienced. Not only were they good and caring people, they were our final link to the last days of Uncle Amer. And I knew we'd never see them again.

12

A Song That Would Like To Make You Cry

BACK IN JORDAN, Dad bought a length of rope and rented a small two-wheeled trailer for hauling the rough box that had been placed in the undertaker's parlor. Someone must have helped Mr. Hawkins carry my uncle up from that cool cellar. He was dressed and laid out with yards and yards of soft packing cloth to keep him from rolling hard against the sides of the pine coffin during our bumpy ride back to the train station. Seeing that we were satisfied with how he had prepared the body, Mr. Hawkins laid down a shroud from head to toe, added more packing cloth, and brought forth a hammer to nail the lid shut. For good measure, he cinched two long straps around each end of the box. While he and Dad took care of financial matters, I helped Mr. Malloy lash the temporary coffin onto the trailer hitched to the stage. Then we left Jordan and retraced the distance back to Forsyth, with Radge sitting next to me. That dog stayed tight by my side for the next ten years. Best dog we ever had.

The other passengers were a man and his wife, expecting a baby any day. Although Jordan had a doctor, the woman insisted on traveling to the hospital in Forsyth where they had relatives. I remember noticing her condition, then looking back at the rough box bouncing along behind the stage on that long, dusty trail. One gone, another on the way.

After dropping the expectant couple off at the hospital, Mr. Malloy delivered Dad and me to the depot in time to book the next train bound for Miles City. From there, we would travel to Chicago, then on to Rockford.

The three of us unloaded the pine coffin and placed it in a small holding room cooled by blocks of ice. Radge laid down on the floor next to the coffin and refused to budge. I stayed with him, then got the idea to rig up a leash from a length of rope tied to the trailer. We joined the others on the platform. Radge took a long drink of water from one of Mr. Malloy's canteens.

Dad settled with our driver, who agreed to return the trailer to Jordan on his next trip back. We shook hands several times, sorry to part company. He told us he felt as bad for Amer as if he were his own brother. Dad offered him five more dollars. At first, Mr. Malloy refused it, but Dad said, "No, that's your'n. You've a right to it."

Although a dollar was hard to come by back then, I was pleased, and proud of my Dad for doing that.

We heard the "All aboard" and had to rush to make sure the coffin got transferred from the holding room to the train's baggage compartment (Amer's dog would ride there, too). We shook hands again and clapped one another on the shoulders, as reluctant in our leave-taking with Mr. Malloy as we were with the McKammans. Even then, he didn't turn his back on us until long after the train had left the station. I watched and waved from the window. We were almost out of sight before I saw him return to his car.

For two days and nights we rode along on the rails, clickety-clack, and when we reached Chicago, discovered there was no branch train scheduled for Rockford until the next day. We had to leave the coffin in another ice-cooled holding room at the depot and take a taxi to the Palmer House hotel. I tied Radge to a stake in the yard behind the kitchen and set out a big bowl of water and table scraps gathered up by the cook. After a light supper, Dad and I fell into bed.

*   *   *

"So there you have it, ladies. When I asked my dad about the funeral plans and about Amer's burial, he said that your folks, Uncle Frank and Uncle Ed, were in charge of the arrangements." I point the stem of my pipe toward the plots across the way. "He was to go in next to Grandma Ernestine and Auntie Edna."

"My, oh, my," says Nellie. "That was some trip for you and Vic."

"Unforgettable is all I can say. Early the next morning, we made sure the pine box was intact and carefully brought aboard the Illinois Central for the last leg of our journey here to Rockford."

"It's certainly too bad your mother and brother couldn't have come for the funeral," says Hannah.

"I wished the same thing. It might have made a difference in how Ray and I got along after that. Oh, we had some fun years together, especially in our twenties. But then he married Eloise and everything went to hell in a hand basket. Now he's in a nursing home. Yep, it's too bad my brother can't be here with us today. At least for the aftermath, in on the telling of my story from beginning to end."

Cal gets up from her place next to the cottonwood tree and brushes off her slacks.

"Wasn't there some way for Gram and Uncle Ray to attend the service?"

"No. It was too big a trip in those days. And costly.

Besides, they couldn't leave the livestock. We had a good-sized dairy herd. Pigs and chickens. A couple of dogs, bunch of cats."

"Yah, yah," says Hannah. "You can't let the animals go even for a day, especially those milk cows."

Using the penknife hooked to my watch chain, I loosen the charred pipe tobacco and tap the bowl against the heel of my shoe. Overhead, the pine boughs and cottonwood leaves are still. Sunshine angles low across the cemetery and reflects off the field of headstones. It's not so warm as when we first arrived. The distant, droning sound of highway traffic has picked up.

"After all these years," I say, glancing at each of my cousins, "just imagine. Ten days from the day he died until the funeral, and Uncle Amer's remains could be shown in all likeness of himself. That undertaker in Jordan may have been strange, creepy even, but he knew his trade. Yessir, Mr. Hawkins did right by Amer."

"May our uncle rest in peace," says Hannah.

She and Nellie rise stiffly, snatch up the handkerchiefs they were sitting on, tuck them into their purses, then shuffle about, a little wobbly, until they can find a balance. Their pastel skirts flutter in a sudden breeze.

Cal gathers Amer's letters for me and reties the bundle with the same soft piece of creamy cotton string that has held them together for seventy years.

"I'm glad we came to Rockford, Dad. And I'm happy that you could tell us all about Amer right here in this cemetery." She grins and cocks her head. "No teacups. No lace doilies."

"I was finally able to get to the end of it, Cal. But it's a hell of a thing to find no marker. And nothing more for Grandma and Auntie."

She hands me the packet of envelopes and points toward the graves. "Well, you've told us their stories. That counts for something."

In an effort to stretch, Nellie staggers backwards in little steps until she can steady herself by gripping the top of the bench.

"Mother and Daddy," she says in a shaky voice, "wondered about Amer's condition. You know, a body traveling such a long distance in that summer heat. Isn't that right, Hannah?"

"Yah, yah. We were surprised at how well he came through. Uncle Vic asked my father to order the very finest metallic casket and a steel grave vault. Our dads took care of that, we'll have you know. As I recall, the funeral was well attended. Wouldn't you say so, Nellie?"

"Oh, yes. The pastor at Aunt Selma's church of worship announced it the Sunday before."

I make it a point to stand up slowly so as not to teeter about like Nellie.

"After the funeral," I explain, placing Amer's letters into my breast pocket, "Dad and I took the last leg of our journey back to Pipestone, then Hadley and the farm. Mother and Ray were relieved to see us, and happy to have another dog on the place. It didn't take Radge long to make friends with Sport and Docky and to start scaring up a few birds, especially when we ran together through the cornrows.

"Did you hear his voice echoing over the fields?" asks Cal, her eyes sparkling.

"What's that?"

"You know. Uncle Amer singing and calling out: 'They're taking off on their own now, boys, so just sit back and watch 'em grow!'"

"Oh, yes. Yes, of course." I give the back of Callie's neck a little squeeze like when she was a girl. "I believe we did, Cal. I do believe we did."

Hannah smiles. "Well, I'd like to know what became of Tom Carmichael."

"He went to trial. Found guilty in the first degree and sentenced to life."

"That's a relief," says Nellie.

"Ah, but he served only two years."

Suddenly I feel as disgusted as I did seven decades ago when we heard that his brothers and father ponied up enough money to bribe the Judge of District Court. That judge arranged for a new trial, this time in Lewiston.

"Tom Carmichael was set free, in spite of the witnesses and earlier testimony. In spite of the fact that Amer's dying declaration could be used as admissible evidence."

"That's awful!" exclaims Nellie.

"Well," says Hannah, "I'm sure the fates eventually took care of Mister Tom Carmichael. That which goes around comes around, don't you know."

"What about Amer's land?" asks Nellie. "Shouldn't it have gone to our folks?"

"Nope. That acreage went back into the Federal registers. He never got the time he needed to prove up on it."

"I can't imagine what we'd do with it, Nellie," says Hannah. "A chunk of land in Eastern Montana? Didn't sound very farmable to me."

"Well, I still say it's a shame." Nellie purses her lips. "Do you think the Carmichaels got it after all?"

"I don't believe so. Of course, we'll never know for sure unless we make the effort to check the records. Anyhow, those Carmichaels are long dead by now."

"Whatever happened to Amer's soddy?"

"I don't know, Nellie. Eventually, I suppose, it crumbled and was plowed back into the earth."

I walk slowly back to Amer's unmarked plot. Hannah follows, then stops to wait for Nellie who has sidled up to Cal as if she's eager to share a secret.

"I didn't want to say this in front of your dad," she

whispers, loudly enough for me to hear, "but I think the main reason our folks didn't bother with a tombstone was that they didn't really approve of...well, you know...how he was and all."

"What do you mean?" Cal looks puzzled.

"Well, you maybe didn't know this about him, but he was always kind of, oh, I don't know. Kind of odd."

"Oh, Nellie," Hannah frowns. "Why don't you just say it. He was a homosexual."

"Isn't the word 'gay'?" asks Nellie.

"Same thing," says Hannah.

My daughter looks stunned, confused, then angry.

"And that's why you never bought a tombstone for him?"

"Well, our folks didn't believe in that sort of thing."

"But he was family, Nellie! Family, for God's sake!"

I stay where I am for a moment, next to the gravesites, proud of my daughter for standing up to this cousin who will never stop parroting her folks. But then I see that Cal is struggling to hold back the tears as her next words tumble out.

"You never knew him. Dad told me all about Uncle Amer, ever since I was a little kid. He played the violin. And he sang Puccini. And he read great books. He had Johnny and Skeeky and a dog named Radge. I read all of his letters. He worked hard for that land. And his soddy? He built that house from dirt. He was a somebody!"

I rush over to ally with my daughter and steer her away from the others. Nellie and Hannah head toward the car, talking loudly, gesturing, scowling back at us, perplexed or bewildered. I'm not sure which.

"Why didn't you ever say anything, Dad, that Amer was gay? I mean, I pretty much figured it out from Nellie's earlier innuendos. This is an important part of who he was."

"We're in his corner, Cal. Always have been."

"But why didn't you ever tell me the whole story? That's why the Carmichaels went after him, wasn't it? It wasn't only about the land."

"In those days, we didn't really have a name for men like that. They were just different, that's all. And a place like Montana back then? Or anywhere out west...."

"My God, what he must have gone through."

"You were pretty young, Cal, when we first talked about Amer. I told you what I knew for sure, what I thought you could understand at the time."

"I guess you've always done that. Measured things out in little doses until you thought I could handle the big picture."

"Are you criticizing the way your mother and I raised you? You and Liz?"

"No, but didn't the rest of his story seem important enough to tell us? At least, later on? That's why he struggled.

That's why he was murdered. I'll bet the sheriff and the courts used the land dispute as an excuse, a cover-up, and didn't do a damned thing to help him. They let it happen."

"He was an easy target, Cal. My folks knew it, but they had to let him go. I'm sure you're right. That his death had more to do with who he was than with his land."

"Which is why the law never protected him, damn their hides."

"We'll never know any of that for sure. Never be able to prove it. As far as I'm concerned, the most important thing was how he lived and struggled to get ahead. He was out there doing the best he could."

With a purpose, Cal walks back to the benches where we'd sat just moments ago and picks a cluster of lavender and yellow wildflowers. We return to the graves for a final look at the ground that must belong to Amer. I open my tobacco pouch and sprinkle a handful of the sweet brown flecks onto the grass next to Cal's little bouquet.

She smiles, seems a bit more relaxed. "You learned that up north, didn't you, Dad?"

"Uh-huh."

I recall writing a letter to Cal and Liz about the afternoon I was invited to smoke the peace pipe with a half dozen men from the Leech Lake Band of Ojibwe. During the ceremony, they paid tribute to the four directions, Mother Earth, Father sky, and the Great Spirit they call Wakan Tanka.

The elder spoke of mankind's responsibilities to others and to the environment. He sprinkled a little tobacco on the ground before placing some in the pipe. "We must give back to Mother Earth a part of what we take," he said.

Then the others spoke and gave colors to the four directions. East is red for the rising sun. South is yellow for the spring bounty. Black stands for the West, after the sun goes down and the spirit world gathers. White stands for the North, where blankets of snow cover the land.

I have always been partial to the East, thanking the Great Spirit for each new day that we're allowed to live upon Mother Earth. Oh, that my uncle had been allowed his full measure on this earth.

Suddenly, from across the years, something the pastor said during Amer's funeral service pops into my head and I recite it for Cal: An evil act took from us a fine man. Yet his existence added to the collective good of mankind. We must understand that the terrible wrong done to him, the way that he died, makes all the more dear the life that was.

"That's beautiful, Dad. I'm surprised you can remember those exact words after all these years."

"Me, too. They just came to me, clear as morning."

"Will you write them down?"

"Yes, Callie girl. I'll do that."

My daughter and I walk the rigid, pebbled path back to the car where Hannah and Nellie are waiting in the back seat. Gravel grates against the soles of our shoes, reminding me of the three-day hike we took to Ocheyedan, Iowa, back when Cal was a youngster—one of our many happy times together.

A short distance away, two young boys are playing hide-and-seek among the steep headstones. We smile at their laughter.

Cal hooks her arm through mine. "We should make another trip, Dad. Buy a marker for the grave, something for your grandma and auntie, too. See that they're all done up right, just as we'd imagined."

"Nope. I won't be coming back."

"Are you sure about that?" she asks, surprised. "You were pretty intent on seeing a stone for Amer."

"Well, here's how I look at it now." I spread my arms wide. "He's everywhere, all around us."

I circle about in a little soft-shoe (a bit slowly, perhaps) to glance back at the graveyard, at the tall pines and cottonwood branches brushing the sky.

"Every time we see trees like these or a field of corn laid by or a slough filled with chattering ducks or hear a tune by Puccini, there he'll be. Besides, Callie girl, I have a hunch you'll be telling Amer's story long after I'm gone. Now isn't that better than some mossy old stone?"

"Dad!" Cal exclaims, stopping in her tracks. "What you just said—that's almost like those lines in *The Grapes of Wrath*.

I don't remember the exact words, but they went something like this:

"Whenever there's a fight so hungry people can eat, I'll be there.... Or a cop beating up a guy.... I'll be in the way kids laugh...when they know supper's ready... An' eat the stuff they raise an' live in the houses they build...."

"I'll be there," I repeat slowly, intent on remembering those words. And glad that my daughter knows them. "I have no more regrets, Cal. Your grandad and I did our part bringing Amer home. He knew he had family that would never fail him."

During the silent drive along these October streets, back to Hannah's house, I grip the steering wheel and picture my uncle's unlabored movements in the fields, his gentle way with the livestock, his thin, yet muscular white legs in rolled up overalls. And then imagine it's a summer afternoon. The sun is hot. We are all lounging together on a grassy slope at the edge of Lake Summit—my father, mother, brother, uncle, and I. And Uncle Amer is singing a song that would like to make you cry.

ACKNOWLEDGMENTS

My thanks for the steady assistance, support, and talent of Nancy Paddock during the process of publishing *A Stone for Amer.* Thanks also to Marly Cornell, Faith Sullivan, Beth Waterhouse, and Ann Woodbeck; and to my dear shelties, Kipp and Cal, who reminded me to take an occasional break from the keyboard.

ABOUT THE AUTHOR

Connie Claire Szarke grew up in southwestern Minnesota, a beautiful prairie land bejeweled with lakes, sloughs, timber, creeks, and wildlife. These, along with the influence of small towns, farming communities, and the people who live there, are integral to the author's work.

Music, a life-long passion, also plays within her stories.

Her award-winning writing has appeared in publications such as *Creekside Poetry, Talking Stick, Dust & Fire, Lake Country Journal Magazine, Community Connections, The Minnesota Project, The Cub of the Golden Lion Passes in Review* for veterans of the 106th Infantry Division/Battle of the Bulge, and *Stories Teachers Tell* (Nodin Press, 2004). Her short story, *StoneWall*, (Red Dragonfly Press, 2012) is set in Ireland.

Szarke's debut novel, *Delicate Armor* (North Star press of St. Cloud, 2012), a Midwest Book Award finalist, is the sequel and companion book to *A Stone for Amer.*

She currently lives on a bay west of Minneapolis.

Please visit ***www.connieclaireszarke.com***.